Items should be returned on or before the last date shown below. Items not already requested by other borrowers may be renewed in person, in writing or by telephone. To renew, please quote the number on the barcode label. To renew online a PIN is required. This can be requested at your local library.
Renew online @ **www.dublincitypubliclibraries.ie**
Fines charged for overdue items will include postage incurred in recovery. Damage to or loss of items will be charged to the borrower.

Leabharlanna Poiblí Chathair Bhaile Átha Cliath
Dublin City Public Libraries

Baile Átha Cliath
Dublin City

Leabharlann Shráid Chaoimhín
Kevin Street Library
Tel: 01 222 8488

Date Due	Date Due	Date Due

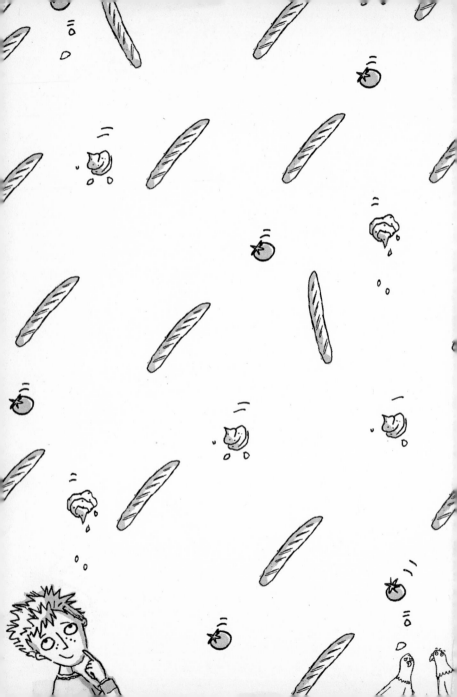

CASPER
CANDLEWACKS

in ATTACK of the BRAINIACS!

First published in Great Britain by HarperCollins Children's Books in 2012
HarperCollins Children's Books is a division of HarperCollinsPublishers Ltd,
77-85 Fulham Palace Road, Hammersmith, London, W6 8JB.

Visit us on the web at
www.harpercollins.co.uk

1

CASPER CANDLEWACKS IN ATTACK OF THE BRAINIACS!
Text copyright © Ivan Brett 2012
Illustration copyright © Hannah Shaw 2012

Ivan Brett and Hannah Shaw assert the moral right to be identified as the
author and illustrator of this work.

ISBN 978-0-00-741159-7

MIX
Paper from
responsible sources
FSC® C007454

FSC™ is a non-profit international organisation established to promote
the responsible management of the world's forests. Products carrying the
FSC label are independently certified to assure consumers that they come
from forests that are managed to meet the social, economic and
ecological needs of present and future generations,
and other controlled sources.

Find out more about HarperCollins and the environment at
www.harpercollins.co.uk/green

CASPER CANDLEWACKS

in ATTACK of the BRAINIACS!

Ivan Brett

Illustrated by Hannah Shaw

HarperCollins *Children's Books*

More adventures with

CASPER CANDLEWACKS

Casper Candlewacks in Death by Pigeon!
Casper Candlewacks in the Claws of Crime!

For Plato, Popper and Pop

Hello

Hello.

You've all heard of the old English tradition of the Village Idiot, right? No? Well then...

There's this age-old law in Britain, passed through Parliament over one million years ago, that decreed the following (translated from caveman): 'Every collection of stone huts shall, at all times, contain one idiot.' It's thought that this law aimed to cheer up the people's boring lives, giving them something to laugh at between sessions of boar-hunting or wheel-inventing.

Fast-forward to the present day and if you visit any English village you'll still find their idiot. Follow the curious smell and muddy footprints, look out for the man in a bobble hat chasing pigeons. Throw him a penny and the rest of your sandwich and thank him for his hard work – people like him are what make Britain great.

But there's one village where things are slightly different. You see, in Corne-on-the-Kobb, a pretty little village with a pretty little cobbled square hidden away in the picturesque Kobb Valley, there isn't an idiot. In Corne-on-the-Kobb there are about two hundred. In fact, every single person who lives in Corne-on-the-Kobb is a magnificently, hilariously wonderful specimen of a village idiot, all apart from one blond-haired scruffy boy called Casper Candlewacks.

Casper is the only non-idiot in Corne-on-the-Kobb, and that's why he's interesting. When an arrogant Italian magician cursed the village, only Casper could un-curse it. When an evil cat burglar stole the village's precious bejewelled sword, only Casper could steal it back. When somebody filled their trousers with custard, only Casper could work the washing machine and tumble dryer and get the trousers back to them, custard free, in under forty-eight hours.

You get the point. Corne-on-the-Kobb is a village of idiots, and that's the way it'll always be. Or is it?

(Yes, it is.)

But is it?

(Yes.)

Look, have you read this book?

(Not yet, no.)

Well, get on with it! You might learn something.

(Sorry. I'll read it now.)

Chapter 1

Bon Voyage

"Lamp? You up yet?" Casper Candlewacks hauled open the corrugated door, flooding the garage with the morning's sunlight. "It's gone half seven and we really shouldn't miss the bus. Not on our first day."

There was a loud bump upstairs as Lamp Flannigan fell out of bed. "Casper?" came the muffled reply. "Where are you? All I can see is carpet."

"You're on the floor, Lamp. Come on, we haven't got long." Casper wriggled in his starched black blazer and loosened his tie. The emblem on Casper's breast pocket showed a snake strangling a bear, with 'SSSS' written below in curly writing. This stood for 'St Simian's School for Seniors' (not the sound the snake was making, as Casper had first thought).

Casper hated the idea of school uniform. Until the start of the summer he'd been at Corne-on-the-Kobb Primary, where the dress code was 'clothes, if you have them'. But, just like Free Envelope Week at the Corne-on-the-Kobb Envelope 'n' Bin Liner MegaMarket, all good things must come to an end. St Simian's demanded a white shirt, black blazer, stiff grey trousers that creased like cardboard and shiny black shoes, all topped off with a mustard-yellow tie. Casper's mum had forgotten about the shoes until last night so she'd dipped his trainers into a tin of black paint. They felt crispy. Casper had had a go at taming his bushy mess of blond hair, but after losing two combs and a metal fork he decided to leave it as it was.

To Casper, Lamp Flannigan's garage felt just like home. He'd spent the whole summer here, building 'Bubbel Buggies' and 'Bluff Boilers' and getting progressively oilier day by day. But a newcomer to the garage would struggle to believe this magical junkyard kingdom was even real. Piles of metal, batteries and raw pasta littered the floor next to boxes filled with wires and bleeping circuit boards. Mad contraptions the shape of armadillos or saxophones (or both) whirred, clicked and honked from every worktop. A pot of smoking silver stuff bubbled away on the edge of a wooden shelf, while a robot with three wheels and a tennis racket for a head trundled in wobbly loops across the floor after a squealing self-bouncing tennis ball. Under a shelf full of wrenches sat a large chicken hutch with a Do Not Disturb sign hanging from the front.

Two things had changed since yesterday. First, there was a new heap of scrap metal in Junk Corner, which was the place Lamp liked to keep his stuff when Bric-a-Brac Basket was full. Along with the usual old tat was a huge blue canister with a nozzle at the top and Helium printed on the front. But the second new thing really captured Casper's attention. A pulsing, wheezing contraption took up most of the space on the workbench, replacing the gearbox filled with jam that had sat

there yesterday, but now sat on the floor, gathering ants. Casper didn't mind; this new machine was miles more exciting than Lamp's jammy gearbox. A set of red bagpipes floated in the air like a tartan zeppelin, tethered in place by several lengths of string reaching up from a heavy iron rack. Strapped tightly round the bagpipes' belly was a bleeping calculator fastened on to a leather belt; the mouthpiece had been extended up into a big yellow bowl that waggled in polite circles above the rest of the machine. The instrument had three wooden pipes, two of which were connected to each other with a length of rubber tube, while the third was taped to the long black neck of a vacuum cleaner that swung about close to the floor like a clumsy tail.

"It cooks omlits," said Lamp. "D'you want one?"

Casper jumped. "Crikey! How did you get down here?"

A short podgy boy with a scrub of soot-black hair and a pear-shaped dongle of a nose stood in the far corner of the garage. In his left hand was a huge red helium balloon; in the other was an anchor on a string. He wore a blazer just like Casper's (except the arms went down to his knees), his trousers were three sizes too small and his tie was made of yellow sofa fabric, looped twice round his neck and knotted in the middle. "I built a lift!" grinned Lamp.

"Ah…" Above Lamp's head there was a hole in the ceiling, just the right size for a large red helium balloon, a boy and an anchor to fit through. "Ahh."

"Look." Lamp let go of the anchor and the balloon lifted him into the air.

Casper giggled. "Come back down here!"

Lamp disappeared through the hole in the ceiling. "Hang on," he called. "I need another anchor." There was some clunking, and a moment later down he floated with a second anchor on a string. "It's for when the stairs are broken," said Lamp, tethering his balloon to a handy knob he'd glued to the wall. "I get through a lot of anchors, though."

"Can't you reuse them?"

Lamp chuckled. "Don't be silly."

"Anyway, what did you say this thing was?" Casper turned back to the captive bagpipes.

"It's my Omlit Gun," smiled Lamp. "It makes lovely omlits and shoots them out here." He waggled the head of the vacuum-cleaner neck in Casper's direction.

Casper ducked, just in case. "Omelettes? I should've guessed." He was used to Lamp's eggy inventions by now. Two months ago Lamp had found Mavis and Bessie, the two egg-laying hens, sitting on his doorstep with a note saying they were his distant cousins. He took them in and gave them a coop, and in return the girls always made sure he had a surplus of eggs to invent stuff with.

The bagpipes let out a weary wheeze.

"So? Does it work?" asked Casper, slightly fearing the answer.

"Dunno," shrugged Lamp. "Let's give it a try. Ladies?"

Mavis and Bessie, Lamp's two prize egg-laying hens and long-distant cousins on his mum's side, popped their rubbery heads out of the coop and clucked sleepily. Mavis, the darker one, flipped over the Do Not Disturb sign with her beak. The other side said The Hens Are In. Please Knock.

Lamp lifted the lid of the hens' coop to pick

out two speckly brown eggs. "Watch this!" He did a little trot on the spot, galumphed over to the Omelette Gun and cracked both eggs into the yellow bowl.

The machine wobbled into motion, a nauseous groan from the belly of the bagpipes tightening into a tuneless wheeze. The strings grew taut, the bag puffed fuller and the eggs slipped down the mouthpiece and out of view. Then the pipes began to whistle a screeching, tuneless tune, a melody of such demonic ugliness that even when Casper blocked his ears, he could smell how bad it sounded.

Lamp did a highland jig around the garage.

The screech rose louder, the bag pumped fuller, the strings stretched and frayed to hold it still, and then when Casper was sure the thing was

about to explode, there was a tremendous rattle as something shot down the vacuum-cleaner neck and spat across the garage, splurging against the far wall and sticking fast.

Casper dared to unblock his ears. "Wow."

Lamp grinned. "Wait for it…"

CHOO!

With a final sneeze, the vacuum cleaner belched a cloud of herbs after the omelette, which filled the air like edible confetti.

Casper could do nothing else but clap. "Amazing!" he cheered. "*Encore!*"

Lamp bowed deeply. "I thank you," he said. "Want one? There's plenty more eggs."

Before Casper could answer, Lamp was already back at the coop, rooting around in the straw. His face crumpled into a frown. "Strange…"

"What's up?"

"I can't find any more eggs. What with the two I've already got this morning that means today they've only laid…" Lamp pulled his arm from the coop and counted up on his fingers, "…six. I mean ten."

"Two," said Casper.

"Exactly. Three. That's the lowest yet."

Apart from the counting part, Lamp was absolutely right. Until a couple of weeks ago, Mavis and Bessie were prize egg-layers. They'd pump out eggs like faulty bubblegum machines, filling their coop right to the top and proudly sitting on the lid. But something had changed because each morning the boys would find fewer and fewer eggs, with no explanation why.

"I don't like this," said Casper suspiciously.

"Maybe they're ill or something."

"Chicken pox?" said Lamp.

"Do chickens get chicken pox?"

"Er, yeah." Lamp clicked his teeth. "Clue's in the name, silly."

Bessie pecked at a little vending machine. It gave a *bloop* and its dispenser scattered a handful of seeds on to the garage floor.

"Come on, Lamp, we've a bus to catch."

"Ooh!" Lamp squealed. "We're going to big boys' school!"

The pit of Casper's stomach wiggled. He wished he shared his friend's enthusiasm, but in truth, he was terrified. Corne-on-the-Kobb wasn't big enough to have its own senior school, so once the kids were old enough, they were shipped off to the sprawling city of High Kobb. You could see its grey towers from the top of the Corne-on-the-Kobb village hall, climbing high into the clouds and beyond, probably into space. Casper had never been to High Kobb, or any city, as a matter of fact. The villagers had told stories and Casper had listened, quivering: the never-ending traffic, murderers on every street corner and giant alligators that crawl out of the sewers and eat your firstborn. Cities struck fear into Casper's heart. And now he had to go to school inside one!

If Casper survived the day, though, he'd have worse waiting for him back in Corne-on-the-Kobb. Tonight was the opening of his dad's brand-new restaurant, an event two months and three kitchen fires in the making. Casper was to be head waiter and mopper of spills, his least favourite job since nappy-recycling.

"Oh, Casper, aren't we gonna have so much fun?"

Casper was jolted back to reality as Lamp stuffed a handful of marbles and an iron into his oil-stained backpack.

"D'you think they have chairs there? Otherwise I'll take this one with me."

"They've already got chairs. I think. Come on, we're going to be late."

"Race you to the bus!" Lamp galumphed out of the garage and veered left down the road.

"This way, Lamp."

"Righty-ho!" He wheeled round and galumphed back into the garage.

Lamp Flannigan was Casper's best friend. He wasn't the fizziest bottle in the fridge in terms of brain power. Directions weren't his strong point, and neither were counting, spelling, herding cattle, walking, breathing, not falling into puddles... Actually, this list is going to continue for an awfully long time. To save money and rainforests it'd be easier to flag up his one and only strong point. Lamp Flannigan was an absolute genius at inventing. He invented the things that nobody in their right mind would ever attempt. But that's the point: Lamp didn't have a right mind. He didn't even have a left mind. He had a sort of slushy heap that mulched around in his skull and gurgled when you shook it. But whatever it was, it sure as beans made him good at inventing. He'd invented telepathic typewriters that type what you think and collapsible caravans that fit into your lunchbox. He'd made rubber paint for bouncy walls and disposable flags that you only wave once. Inventing wasn't just Lamp's hobby, it was his life.

Casper walked through the park with Lamp trotting behind him, stopping every so often to sniff a flower or re-Velcro his shoes.

At the entrance to the village square sat Casper's dad's brand-new restaurant, The Battered Cod. There were about two weeks' worth of jobs to do before The Battered Cod was ready to open, which was fine, except that tonight was the opening night.

Ting-a-ling.

"Casp!" The balding head of Julius, Casper's dad, popped out of the front door like a hairy egg, but without much hair. "Glad I found you. Can you help me with this oven? It's still in bits, and Cuddles ate the manual."

"Sorry, I can't. The bus leaves any minute."

"Bus? Where d'you think you're going on a

school day, young man?"

"School, Dad. St Simian's, remember?"

"Oh yes." Julius scratched his scalp. "Course I remember. Well, have fun. I'll just do the oven myself, then."

"Good luck," Casper grimaced. He wouldn't normally leave his dad alone with an oven, even though he was a chef. "Don't... explode... or anything."

"I'll try not to."

"Hi, Mister Candlewacks," piped up Lamp.

"Hi, Lamp." Julius waved and disappeared back into his restaurant.

Ting-a-ling.

(One thing Julius *had* fixed was the thing that went *ting-a-ling* when you opened or closed the door. It's a very important piece of equipment, particularly to deter robbers, who are generally terrified of bells.)

The village square was packed that morning with weeping mothers and trembling children standing by a huge train carriage lashed to a green tractor. It was the closest thing to a school bus Corne-on-the-Kobb could muster, but it didn't half look grand there, grumbling away on the cobbles. In the centre of the square stood the massive gleaming stone statue of Mayor Rattsbulge, clutching his bejewelled sword in one hammy fist.

The real Mayor Rattsbulge stood in the shadow of his chiselled stone twin, twice as fat, not nearly as handsome, and clutching a sausage rather than a sword. The statue had been finished two weeks ago, and every day since, the mayor had stood proudly beside it, pointing it out to passers-by and loudly telling them how accurate it was.

Other villagers trotted across the cobbles on their morning errands, waving at each other and giving their mayor a wide berth. Betty Woons – a sprightly 107-year-old – whizzed in skittering circles across the square in her turbo-powered wheelchair, running over so many toes that she lost count and had to start again; village gardener Sandy Landscape leant against a wall, chatting to a hedge; bent-backed Mrs Trimble tugged at the nine leads attached to the collars of nine stubborn cats that licked their paws and meowed throatily; and four-foot-tall pub landlord Mitch McMassive puffed and wheezed as he tried once more to roll an enormous beer barrel towards The Horse and Horse, only for it to roll backwards and flatten him against the cobbles.

Casper and Lamp passed through the crowd, bumping into a grubby little man with a pinched face hidden under his grubby black beret.

"Hullo, Mr Renée!" Lamp said.

"'Allo, boys," growled Renée in his thick French drawl. He grinned, his rubbery lips parting to reveal a few brown teeth. In the corner of his mouth hung a soggy, thin cigarette that wobbled as he talked. Renée's gaze settled on Casper, and Caspar shivered.

"Hi," Casper said briskly. He didn't know why Renée made his skin crawl like that. He wasn't a cruel man, just a little cold. Renée had come to Corne-on-the-Kobb from France a couple of months ago. Quite why he'd done that, nobody had bothered to ask. None of the other villagers paid the poor chap the slightest bit of attention because he was French. (The people of Corne-on-the-Kobb were scared of two things: foreigners and dinosaurs. Renée was at least one of those.)

"How's your cheese shop getting along?" asked Casper politely.

"Ah, not bad, not bad," nodded Renée. "I think it will be making quite ze splash."

"Why?" Lamp scratched his hair. "Is it wet?"

Renée frowned and reached for the little English dictionary he'd taken to keeping in a pocket. "I, er, do not…"

"Don't worry, sir," said Casper, motioning for Renée to put his dictionary away. "He just means to say how excited we are about tasting all your cheese."

"Heh," said Renée, breaking into a gruff smile. "Yes. Ze cheese." He winked at Lamp and turned to shuffle away.

Casper turned to Lamp and saw that he was grinning. "What was that wink?"

"Huh?"

"ALL ABOARD, TICKETS 'N' RAILCARDS, MIND THE GAP!" shouted Sandy Landscape, clambering up the side of his tractor. "TRAIN NOW STANDIN' ON PLATFORM ONE'S THE TEN PAST EIGHT TER HIGH KOBB."

As children tottered up on to the train carriage and mothers wailed ever louder, Casper's nerves flooded back in and stung him like a mouthful of seawater. What waited for him at the other end of this journey? Did High Kobb really have alligators? Would he even make it home to see the opening of The Battered Cod?

The 'bus' roared into life, pumping black fumes and a sleeping hedgehog out of the exhaust pipe and into the crowd. The tractor shunted forwards and the carriage jerked into motion behind, throwing the children back in their seats. The villagers cheered, tearful mothers waved their hankies and little children and dogs chased the carriage down the road, although it wasn't going very fast so they just stood there and wondered what to do once they'd caught up with it.

At the back of the crowd, Renée shuffled away across the cobbles. He stopped at the door to a boarded-up shop with a small sign that said Le Cheese Shop. He open tonight. He fiddled with the key, pushed open the door and shuffled inside. But that's not important because Renée's obviously not anyone to worry about and he's certainly not hatching any evil plans or anything. Don't even know why I mentioned him, actually.

Chapter 2

Big Boys' School

The country lanes trawled by slower than a lazy snail. Casper smudged his nose on the window of the train and sighed. Summer was over and school was ready to take its place, filling his days with boredom and sums.

Casper and Lamp sat at one of those four-seat tables opposite Milly and Milly Mollyband, the identical twins (who'd been given the same name to save time and name-badges). They'd obviously heard about the alligators too because they both trembled so hard that Lamp thought there was an earthquake going on.

Eventually, Lamp decided he liked earthquakes, so Casper had some more time to look out of the window. When he looked back, Lamp was scratching his oily black hair and then sniffing his finger. "Strawberry," he said. "Must be Monday."

Casper frowned. "What?"

"I invented a shampoo that knows what day it is. It changes flavour to match. Monday means strawberry."

"Oh…" Casper frowned.

"And you know I smelt of eggs yesterday?"

"Was that the shampoo too?"

"Nope, I'd just been eating them. Got my last

three here. Want one?" He pulled three boiled eggs from an inner pocket of his blazer.

Casper took an egg to keep Lamp happy and placed it carefully in his backpack.

Lamp licked his lips and saved his two for later.

"OY! WOSSAT?" A shriek tore from the back of the carriage.

"It's Anemonie!" whispered Casper. "What does she want?"

"I want that! It's mine!" A small, pointy-nosed girl with squinty eyes and dark hair stomped up the aisle, pointing straight at Lamp with her sharpened pink fingernails. Her sickly sweet perfume made Casper gag.

Lamp plunged his eggs into his pocket and pretended to be asleep.

"What were you holding? Give it."

"Zzzzzz," snored Lamp. Then he opened one eye and whispered, "Has she gone yet, Casper?"

Anemonie Blight jabbed a few fingernails into Lamp's side.

"Ouch! I mean… zzz. Oh, bother." The game was up.

"Give it." Anemonie reached for a sharp-tipped pencil that she kept behind her ear. "Last warning, Flannigan. This pencil is leaded."

"Fine. Didn't want it, anyway." Lamp withdrew his trembling hand from the pocket clutching one of the boiled eggs.

"An *egg*?" Anemonie's face wrinkled with disgust. She swatted the egg at Milly Mollyband, but it missed and struck Milly Mollyband.

Anemonie snarled. "Now, gimme your lunch money."

"That was my lunch," said Lamp, staring hungrily at Milly Mollyband's blazer.

"How 'bout yours, then, Candlewacks?" Anemonie swung the pencil towards Casper.

Casper considered giving Anemonie his egg as well, but he valued not having a pencil sticking out of his face a bit too much for that. The two one-pound coins that he'd brought for lunch weighed heavily in his pocket. Begrudgingly, he handed them over.

"There. Not so hard, was it?" Anemonie smiled her sickly smile and skipped away back down the carriage to play 'Ding Dong Bell' on Teresa Louncher's pigtails.

Casper sighed. Anemonie had been stealing his lunch money for as long as he could remember, but for some reason he thought going to senior school would change things.

One of Teresa's pigtails landed on his table with a *plap*. Evidently things hadn't changed.

"I miss my egg," moaned Lamp.

"Here. Have mine." Giving Lamp his egg back cheered him hugely. He sang some jolly songs until he ran out of breath, and then he went blue because he forgot to breathe in again, so Casper had to remind him.

The road bent round and Casper caught his first sight of High Kobb – an ugly mass of grey towers and belching chimneys scarring the beautiful landscape like a scab on a princess.

As the country roads became paved streets, Casper longed to be home again. The endless dusty concrete and nose-to-tail traffic made his heart sink. Luckily he saw no alligators in the gutters and the people walking the streets looked like businessmen, not murderers. But their business might have been murdering people, so Casper didn't fully relax.

The tractor turned a corner and rolled up through a pair of massive wrought-iron gates, grinding to a halt inside a drab concrete playground full of pupils dressed in black blazers and yellow ties.

"My new kingdom!" screeched Anemonie. "Move outta the way, I'm getting off first." She barged Ted Treadington aside with a well-placed elbow, and the rest of the kids scurried out of the aisle to let her pass.

Anemonie jumped down the steps and landed with her arms outstretched on the tarmac. "All right, boys and girls, listen up or I'll spread you on my toast. The name's Anemonie Blight and I'm in charge here."

The High Kobb kids ran about, skipping and jumping and paying absolutely no attention.

"I SAID LISTEN!" Anemonie's face swelled redder.

Casper, Lamp and the bolder Corne-on-the-Kobb kids tiptoed off the carriage and stood behind Anemonie.

Sixteen older kids whooshed past after a football, creating a small hurricane that blew over Milly and Milly Mollyband.

"YOU BOYS. STOP IT! I'M ANEMONIE BLIGHT! I'M ANEMONIE BLIGHT! LISTEN TO ME!"

A scruffy little boy came flying through the air and crunched to the ground at Anemonie's feet.

Anemonie screamed.

Casper dashed forward and shoved Anemonie out of the way. The boy looked pretty dazed. "Are you OK?"

"Casper," gasped Lamp, "did you see that? They can fly in big boys' school!"

The boy had short, shaven hair and a bony little face. His uniform was made of faded baggy hand-me-downs and there was a cut on his lip. He blinked a few times and then his eyes focused on Casper. "I'm f-f-fine. Just playing r-rugby."

Casper frowned. "Then why were you—"

"I was the b-ball."

"Oh."

"Not my f-f-favourite position," the boy said. "The B-brewster b-brothers chose it."

"The Brewster brothers?"

"You're n-not from r-round here, are you?" Wincing, the boy made his way to a standing position. "My name's S-snivel. I know what you're finking. S-stupid name."

"It's not that stupid," said Casper. "He's called Lamp."

Lamp waved.

"And I'm Casper." Casper went to shake Snivel's hand, but he jumped back, terrified. "Don't worry, I only wanted to shake hands."

Snivel stared at Casper's hand. "Yeah, s-s-sorry. I'm n-not used to…"

There was an awkward shuffling while everyone worked out where to put their hands. Casper put his in his pockets and Lamp put his in Casper's bag, but then Lamp wanted them back and couldn't remember where he'd left them, so Casper had to take off his bag to find them for him.

All the while at the side of the group, Anemonie was desperately screeching commands at three girls and a skipping rope. The three girls and the skipping rope just laughed and carried on skipping.

"W-what's wrong with her?" Snivel pointed at Anemonie.

"She's used to being in charge," sighed Casper.

"Y-yeah, sh-she's not got a chance here. Not with the B-b-brewster b-brothers around."

"But who *are* the Brewster brothers?"

A look of fear sketched itself across Snivel's face. "Well, they're b-big, and they r-run the place…"

"Like Mayor Rattsbulge," said Lamp.

"…and they'll t-take your l-lunch money…"

"So will Mayor Rattsbulge," said Lamp.

"…and there's f-f-four of them."

"Like Mayor Rattsbulge," said Lamp. "Except there's only one of him."

"THERE 'E IS!" Four enormous brutes with

shaved heads and tiny foreheads, their sleeves rolled up to reveal hairy, tree-trunk arms, shoved through the crowd straight towards Snivel.

Anemonie spun round, opened her mouth, realised they were twice her size and closed it again.

"Brewster brothers?" whispered Casper.

"Yep." Snivel was trembling. "And… erm… unless you want to b-be a r-rugby ball, you should r-really r-r-r—"

Casper guessed the rest of the word and dashed off across the playground, followed by Snivel and the rest of the terrified class, some screaming, some whimpering, one sneezing. (Ted Treadington was allergic to playgrounds.) Lamp considered becoming a rugby ball for a second, but then decided he preferred football, so he galumphed along behind.

"They're huge!" shouted Casper as he ran down a plasticky-smelling corridor beside Snivel. "What have they got against you?"

"Erm…" Snivel had quite small legs so he had to run twice as fast. "You all f-first years?"

"Yeah. But what about—"

"M-me too. We've got geography."

Casper groaned.

Teresa Louncher tripped over a Mind the Step sign and clattered to the floor. Casper picked her up, but she was crying too hard to carry on, so he hid her in a locker and promised to find her at break.

"It's j-just up here." Snivel guided them to the left into an identical corridor, up some stairs, through a heavy door and into a dull classroom with maps plastered all over the walls and ceiling.

The children collapsed into seats and caught

their breath. It looked like the Brewster brothers hadn't followed. In fact, given that there were quite a few children flying past their window and that they were on the second floor, Casper felt quite sure they were still outside.

"I don't like big boys' school any more," huffed Lamp. "Can we go home now?"

Snivel was nervously watching through the glass of the classroom door.

"They knew you, Snivel," said Casper, clutching the stitch in his side.

"Y-yeah…" muttered Snivel.

"But it's only the first day. How did that happen so fast?"

Nervously, Snivel stuck out his pale little hand. "N-name's S-s-snivel. S-snivel B-brewster. I've n-never shaken h-hands before."

Chapter 3

Five Brewsters and a Brainiac

"They're your brothers?" Casper shook his head. "But you're so…"

"S-small?"

"Well, no. But I mean, compared to them."

"I know. I'm the r-runt."

The door burst open and everyone screamed, which made the skinny woman standing in the doorway scream even higher and cower behind her register. After a few tense moments she peeked out, saw no monsters and squeaked with relief. She had long brown hair and a mousy face that squeezed to a tip at her chin.

"Sorry. Hello, class; sorry." The woman tiptoed to the teacher's desk and sat low in the spinny chair, hiding as much of herself as she could behind a small stack of books.

"There you are, Lady!" shouted Lamp, bouncing up and down and pointing at the shivering stack of books. "I found you. Is it my turn to hide now?"

Casper grabbed Lamp just as he made for the nearest loose floorboard. "Come on, Lamp, time to sit down." They found their way to some desks at the front.

The woman spoke quietly, to the floor rather

than the class. "Sorry… erm… my name's Miss Valenteen. I'm your geography teacher. If that's OK. Sorry." She opened the register with shaking fingers and called the first few names. "Daryl Ablebody?"

"Yes, miss."

"Margarine Bannister?"

"Yes, miss."

"Anemonie Blight?"

"Hmph."

Casper glanced around for Anemonie, confused as to why she wasn't terrorising Miss Valenteen already. This was the sort of teacher she'd usually eat for breakfast. (Not literally, of course. Anemonie's breakfast was a bowl of Sickly-Pops with pink food colouring in the milk.) There she was, sitting at the back of the class with crossed arms and the sulkiest face since the village shop ran out of pink food colouring.

Miss Valenteen had stopped at the next name, her mouth too scared even to say the words. "Snivel," – her teeth chattered – "Snivel B-brewster?"

"Y-yes, miss."

Her eyes darted to Snivel. She frowned. "You're the new Brewster boy?"

"Y-yes."

"Oh, thank goodness for that." Miss Valenteen's shoulders sagged, her head dropped back, her mouth broke into a broad grin. "Well, that's OK, then. I thought you were another of those ghastly Brewster brothers. But look at you! You couldn't hurt a fly! Right, then." She stood up, swept aside her book barrier and carried on as relieved as the fly currently buzzing round Snivel Brewster's head. "Casper Candlewacks?"

"Yes, miss."

Without the threat of a Brewster, Miss Valenteen continued the lesson a new woman. She sang the rest of the register and then tangoed round the classroom handing out textbooks.

As Casper watched poor Snivel set out his hand-me-down pencils next to his hand-me-down pencil sharpener, he felt a pang of pity. Imagine having to follow in the footsteps of the Brewster brothers. Your legs would get achy just trying to keep up, for starters.

Miss Valenteen clapped her hands. "OK, class, we'll start with a geography test."

"Oh no," moaned Lamp, "I don't even know where geography *is*."

"Question one: what's the capital of Mongolia?"

Lamp's hand shot up.

"Yes?"

"Ulaanbaatar, miss. Population of just over a million, lying one thousand, three hundred and ten metres above sea level."

"Well… yes!" said Miss Valenteen. "One point to you."

There was a long pause, broken by a *donk* noise as Casper's jaw hit the ground.

Lamp looked shocked, and quite rightly. He touched his lips with a doubting finger. Had those words really just come out of his mouth?

Miss Valenteen continued. "Question two: where is Brazil, and why?"

Lamp's hand was the first up again. "The eastern side of South America, miss. It's there because of continental drift caused by plate tectonics."

"Right again! Two points to you."

Lamp gazed at Casper in open-mouthed glee. "Did you see me do that?" he gasped. Lamp had never got more than one point on a test before (and that was in art when the task was 'Draw your best impression of an ink splodge').

The lesson went on, Lamp's hand carried on shooting up and up, collecting points like a reckless driver in a speed-camera factory. The rest of the class didn't stand a chance. Soon Casper's mind drifted to the evening that lay ahead – opening night at The Battered Cod, two hundred demanding diners and a whole heap of washing-up. What if his dad blew up another oven? What if Cuddles threw another tantrum? What if Mayor Rattsbulge ate another table? The possibilities were too horrifying to consider.

Just as Lamp secured his forty-third point by solving the famine problem in Africa, the door slammed open and four burly young men, muscles stacked up to their chins, stomped through.

"LUNCH MUNNY!" shouted the biggest one.

The Brewster brothers had arrived.

All round Casper the terrified children hid behind their hands. Miss Valenteen dived under her desk with a squeal.

"S-stay calm," whispered Snivel. "If you don't m-move, they c-can't see you."

The Brewsters tromped round the classroom, collecting loose change in a bucket. Lamp proudly presented his Brewster an egg and found it stuffed into his mouth (which was fine by him).

"The b-biggest one's Bash," whispered Snivel. "Then there's Spit, Clobber and P-pinchnurse."

Casper frowned. "Pinchnurse?"

"W-we're named after the first fing we do after we're born. I s-snivelled. P-pinchnurse pinched a nurse."

A Brewster, with one fat caterpillar of an

eyebrow, stopped at Snivel's table. "Lunch munny."

"Clobber, it's m-me."

"You what?" A glimmer of recognition crossed Clobber's eyebrow. "Pocket munny."

As Snivel emptied his pockets, a shadow loomed over Casper's desk, the fetid stench of hot-tuna breath filling his nostrils.

"Lunch munny."

Trembling, Casper looked up. The biggest Brewster of all, the one Casper guessed was Bash, towered above him, his toothless grin and shrunken forehead punctuating a face that looked almost entirely like a bruised potato.

"I…" trembled Casper, "I d-don't have any."

Bash leant even closer. "Lunch munny," he whispered, the tuna stink singeing Casper's nose-hairs.

"I promise, I don't have any! I've already given it to her." Casper pointed at Anemonie and was relieved to find the biggest Brewster's eyes searching for the point's target.

"He's lying! Don't listen to hURRK—" Anemonie Blight was lifted upside down by a bushy-nose-haired Brewster and shaken around by her feet, loosening all the cash hidden in the lining of her blazer. Then she was dumped in a corner with all the other empties.

Bash scowled at Casper. "Tomorrah, you bring dubble."

Casper nodded vigorously.

The brute pointed to his eyes and then Casper's eyes and then to his own fist, which meant something vaguely threatening and dangerous, but Casper wasn't quite sure what.

After the whole class had been done and Miss Valenteen had written out a cheque, Bash thanked everybody for their time and led his brothers away to the next classroom.

"S-sorry," said Snivel. "You d-don't want to m-make Bash angry."

Casper smiled weakly. "I'll try not to. How have you lasted this long?"

"Q-quite a lot of h-hiding."

The lesson continued as before, except that

Miss Valenteen was back to her shaky self. Lamp racked up goodness-knows-how-many points, a gold star and the Nobel Prize for Literature, while Casper and the rest of the class looked on agape.

When the bell rang, the kids skittered out of the room and down the corridor, peeping round each corner for Brewsters.

"How d'you do that back there, Lamp?" asked Casper.

Lamp shrugged. "Dunno. I think I was just lucky."

"You can't have just been lucky seventy-six times in a row!"

"Seventy-seven, actually."

Next lesson was music, where Lamp played a faultless rendition of Beethoven's First Piano

Concerto on a tiny xylophone.

At lunch, Snivel was recruited by his brothers for a cricket match (he played the stumps). Casper and Lamp watched at the boundary, wincing every time one of the Brewsters was bowled out. Casper tried to recite The Battered Cod's menu to Lamp from memory, but it got really tiring really fast after Lamp starting reciting it back to Casper in Latin.

In English, Lamp finished the grammar worksheet before Mr Falstaff could hand it out, and then in religious studies, he disproved three religions only to create four more.

The bus home was a sombre affair for everyone apart from Lamp. His blazer was covered in gold stars, so he was pretending to be the night sky.

"Look, Casper! This is Ursa Minor, and that's the Big Dipper." He marked out the shapes of the constellations with an excited finger. "And this is the Swallowing Donkey, and this one doesn't have a name yet, so I'll call it Trevor."

Halfway home, Casper remembered that Teresa Louncher was still stuck in that locker. He swore he'd remember to let her out tomorrow.

On the back seat, Anemonie nibbled her fingernails and growled at anybody who came too close. She'd never been anything but Queen of the Classroom before (except once, when she declared herself Holy Empress of the Playground and got Ted Treadington to build her a temple out of lunchboxes). But now she was nothing more than a lowly peasant at the Court of Lord Brewster. That sort of thing stung.

"Can I come round?" asked Lamp. "I can't remember where I left my house."

"Not tonight. We're doing the grand opening of The Battered Cod. You coming?"

"Will there be food?"

"It's a restaurant. Of course there'll be food."

"Because I love it when there's food."

Chapter 4

The Battered Cod

The tractor ground to a halt in Corne-on-the-Kobb's village square and Sandy Landscape bellowed, "'Ere we are, kiddies, 'ome an' dry, safe an' sound, bread an' drippin'. Don't leave yer berlongin's on the bus unless it's sammiches." The children tumbled out through the carriage door and scampered off home to cuddle their mummies. Lamp shuffled off with an eager wave, leaving

Casper almost alone in the square.

Sitting on the step by the boarded-up cheese shop was that grubby Frenchman Renée, sucking on a tiny grey cigarette.

Casper waved.

"'Allo, boy." His fat lips curled into a smile. "Are you being ready for… er… ze large evening?"

Casper nodded. The fact that Renée's cheese shop was opening on the same night as his dad's restaurant had been a worry, but not for long. The villagers liked cheese, but only when it came in heavy yellow bricks. French cheese, with all its liquid middles and herby crusts and *essence de cowshed*, would not appeal to the villagers one morsel.

Through the window of The Battered Cod, Casper could see Julius Candlewacks teetering on a ladder, grasping for a massive wonky lampshade that hung just out of reach.

"Better go and help," grimaced Casper.

"Ah, *c'est bon*. Say 'allo to your fazzer."

Casper trotted the rest of the way across the square.

Ting-a-ling.

"Dad?" Casper pushed open the restaurant door, caught the corner of the ladder and sent it toppling over, leaving Julius Candlewacks hanging from the lampshade.

"Help!" Julius flailed his legs about and suddenly realised he was terrified of heights. "I can't hold on! I'm too young to die!"

"Just jump. It's not far."

"It's miles! I'll break my legs! Get me a parachute or something."

"We don't have a—"

RRRRIPPPP went the lampshade and, along with Julius, it tumbled to the carpet.

Julius checked he was alive, breathed a sigh of relief and then noticed how far the bit of lampshade in his hands was from the rest of the lampshade. "Oh."

"Sorry, Dad."

"It's fine!" He sprang to his feet with forced jollity. "It's modern. Half a lampshade is the new lampshade. Soon everyone'll be doing it. Now, plenty to do." And he tottered off to look at the list of unfinished jobs scribbled all over the Today's Specials blackboard.

It had just gone four o'clock, which left three hours until opening time.

"How can I help?" asked Casper.

"Right," Julius read down the list. "You need to connect that oven, peel the spuds, get a new fridge, sweep up the old fridge, label the meat pile and fix the lock on the loo. Got that?"

Casper groaned.

Ting-a-ling.

"Caspy!" Casper's mother, Amanda Candlewacks, burst through the restaurant door. She had long blonde hair, scratches all over her face and a wriggling baby in a bag slung over one shoulder. "Look at me, Caspy, I'm a real mother!"

"How was your first day with Cuddles?"

"Wonderful! We went to the park, she caught some squirrels, I lost her down the back of the tumble dryer—"

The baby screeched and thrashed about, gnashing its razor-sharp teeth. This was Cuddles,

Casper's sister, the least cuddly baby since Clemmie Answorth adopted a cactus. (The cactus didn't last long, by the way. It was eaten by Cuddles, along with Clemmie Answorth's shoes and purse and Don't Eat my Cactus sign.)

"But I think she might be broken. Can you take a look at her, darling?" Amanda smiled sweetly at Casper.

It didn't take long to see, or to smell, what was going on. "Mum, her nappy's full. Like every day. You just need to change her."

"Change her?" Amanda's brow furrowed in confusion. "But I like this one."

"Not all of her, Mum. Just the nappy."

"How do I do that?"

"I showed you yesterday."

"But I need to do it today," she giggled.

Casper sighed and laid Cuddles out on Table 4. His mum wasn't a quick learner. She wasn't even a slow learner. As it turned out, Amanda Candlewacks wasn't a learner at all. What's more, she was about eleven years late to this 'mothering' malarkey, and she couldn't seem to get the hang of it. But today, with Casper going to school, Amanda was faced with her first full day of unaided mothering.

"All done," said Casper, fastening the pin extra tightly. "And stop putting her in bags."

"How else will I carry her? Some sort of trolley?" She burst into trills of fruity laughter.

"Yes, Mum. They call it a buggy."

"Well, I call it a waste of money. If a bag's good enough for my shopping, it's good enough for my daughter. Anyway, I'm shattered. Your turn to look after her now!"

"No, Mum, I'm—"

"Thanks, Caspy, you're a star." Amanda collapsed where she stood and was snoring before she hit the floor.

"Great."

Cuddles gnawed on her own foot.

Casper left Cuddles to peel the potatoes (her fangs were perfect for the job) and clomped

through to the kitchen. Last week Julius had bought every single item from the *Kitchens 'n' More* catalogue, and now the whole lot was squeezed into his minuscule new kitchen. Four-slot toasters were stacked on top of chrome-finished deep-fat fryers, all still wrapped in plastic and far from being plugged in. In fact, nothing was plugged in because the only thing Julius *had* forgotten was something to plug them all into. Until further notice the kitchen would be lit by dozens of torches hanging from the ceiling or propped up in mugs.

"Right," said Julius from behind a stack of flat-pack shelving units. "Block your ears!"

Casper did as he was told, and just in time too, because the next moment a deafening buzz rocked the room. Casper dived behind the oven just before hundreds of knives jiggled from their rack and

79

thunked to the linoleum floor where he'd been standing, sticking fast.

"DAD!" he bellowed. "WHAT ARE YOU DOING?"

The noise stopped. Julius blew a cloud of sawdust from the tip of his power-drill like a spy with a smoking gun. "Drilling holes."

"What for?"

"Electricity. This wall goes through to the restaurant so I'm sticking a wire through."

"Just watch where you're drilling. There're water pipes and all sorts in there."

"Trust me, Casp. I've done this before." He winked and flipped down his goggles, then the drill roared into action again. The room shook, the wall wobbled, torches dropped from the ceiling and mugs rolled off tables, plunging the kitchen into darkness, but still Julius drilled on.

"DAD, STOP!" yelled Casper, but for all Julius could hear he might as well have been making farmyard noises.

And then, with a *BRRRROOOOOO*, he'd drilled through. A shaft of clean light shone from the restaurant.

"Fantastic!" cheered Julius, standing back to admire his work.

"You sure the wall's OK?" Casper didn't claim to be an expert, but he was sure he'd read somewhere that walls weren't meant to wobble.

"Solid as a rock, Casp." Julius banged on the wall twice and the plaster gave way round his hand. Then a large chunk crumbled off and the whole right side toppled inwards. Casper dived for cover again as an avalanche of wall imploded around him. Dust and rubble filled his lungs, his eyes stung and he finally got to find out what plaster tasted like. (Not bad, a bit bland, 6/10.)

The dust settled. Casper dared to peek out from his hiding place. A grey Julius-shaped statue stood in place of the wall. The kitchen and the restaurant were no longer two rooms, they were one room. A room filled with rubble. Amanda's snoring and Cuddles's gnawing were the only noises Casper could hear. Then the Julius-shaped statue coughed a cloud of dust.

Casper fumbled for some consoling words. "Dad, I—"

"Open plan!" Julius's grey face broke into a grin. "We'll be open plan." He tottered between kitchen and restaurant, holding imaginary plates of food. "Ketchup, madam? Why, of course!"

He pranced back into the kitchen, picked up an imaginary bottle and pranced back to the table again. "See, Casper? It's that easy now."

Casper smiled timidly.

A gravelly cough came from the other side of the restaurant and then, in a rough French drawl, "I will… er… be coming back later?"

Julius screamed. It was the Frenchman.

"Renée! Didn't notice you come in! Must fix the *ting-a-ling*-er. Anyway, come on in, take a seat. I think there's one under this wall."

Renée didn't sit down. Instead he sucked on his stick-thin cigarette and chewed the smoke. "'Allo, Julius, *mon ami*. But what is all zis?"

"Oh, it's nothing." Julius kicked some rubble under a table, but it just crumbled under his foot. "Just making some final… adjustments. All ready for tonight?"

Renée shrugged nonchalantly. "Meh, I not worry about zat."

"Well, we're right behind you. Isn't that right,

Casp?" Julius grinned at Renée with a few too many teeth. "We think it's just great that you're over here in Britain. You know to ask if you need anything."

"Zat is most kind." Renée bowed. "I am still, how you say, getting under ze grippings with zis country. Ze cheese, he is my passion."

"Oh, me too. We all love cheese here, especially when it's blue or smelly and not just a heavy yellow brick." Julius nudged Casper, so he nodded vigorously.

"Ah, I must not be staying for long. I am only here for to invite you. You will come to ze opening night of my… er… shop of ze cheese?"

Julius's laugh had a touch of pity. "Renée, my friend, how many times? I can't join you tonight – my restaurant's opening too."

Renée turned to leave, flashing a dirty yellow smile from under his beret. "*Oui*, Julius, but you will come." He trotted into the square without a goodbye.

Ting-a-ling.

"What was that last bit about?" Casper scratched his head.

Julius stared into the middle distance with a frown, as if there was some distant memory tickling the very edge of his mind. He shook his head and plodded off to find a broom. "Lots to do, Casper!" he yelled over his shoulder. "How are those spuds? As soon as this oven's on, I need to get them roasting."

A screech and a burp from the corner of the restaurant meant that Cuddles had finished her job. Casper picked his way over the rubble towards Table 4.

"Oh, Cuddles. You haven't."

Cuddles grinned, victory in her sticky little eyes. She'd peeled the potatoes all right – in fact she'd done it perfectly. In front of her was a bowl full of beautiful paper-thin peelings. But the potatoes were nowhere to be seen. She sneezed, spraying Casper's face with a fine mashed-potato mist.

"Casper?" yelled Julius. "I need those spuds."

"Yeah, about the spuds…" His mouth was dry, his face wet and the carpet covered in wall. How much worse could today get?

Well, if you really want to know – much, much worse…

Chapter 5

Best Served Cold

Casper's afternoon faded to evening as preparations continued in The Battered Cod. Seven o'clock thundered ever closer like an angry bull towards a picnic. By six, the kitchen was all plugged in (at the expense of Julius's eyebrows, singed off by a small gas leak and a naked flame) and the food was on its way.

Julius had decided that the restaurant's

theme was *Best of British*: classic British dishes cooked in that unique Candlewacks style. He'd been toying with the idea of Thai food for a while, but Mrs Trimble's village shop had sold out of lemongrass and Julius's attempt to milk a coconut had ended in three smashed windows and a big dent in the middle of next-door's greyhound.

Best of British it was, then, but to Julius's credit, he'd done a great job. He'd cooked up *Bangers and Mash in a Red Leicester Letterbox*; *Slow-roast Cricket Bat*; *Double-decker Cucumber Sandwiches* painted with *Home-ketchupped Tomatoes* to look like buses; *Tea-flavoured Scones* and *Scone-flavoured Tea*; *Beefeaters' Hats filled with Juicy Ground Beef* and a massive *Shepherd's Pie* in the shape of the Queen.

Julius plopped countless battered fish, battered sausages and one misplaced battered plimsoll into the vat of bubbling oil. He snatched a look at the clock and yelped. "Five minutes! What's it like out there?"

Casper dared to peek through the front window to the village square. At least half the village milled about outside, squishing their noses against the restaurant window to get a good view. "Busy, Dad."

"Brilliant!" He clapped his hands and grinned, then wrestled Cuddles away from a tray of Yorkshire puddings. "Right, Casper, let's get ready. Knives and forks, clean cups, salt and vinegar on every table. Amanda! You ready?"

"Yes, CHEF!" Amanda squeaked, like she'd seen them do on telly. Amanda danced around behind her cocktail bar, plopping three teabags down the neck of a bottle of gin and uncorking the brown sauce.

Casper saw the mob and hiccupped. Idiots lumbered at the glass like a hoard of ravenous zombies. Right at the front, pressed up against the creaking door, was the enormously fat mayor of Corne-on-the-Kobb, Mayor Ignatius P. Rattsbulge.

"LET US IN!" Mayor Rattsbulge bellowed, licking his blubbery lips in speedy circles.

"I can't hold them back much longer, Dad."

"But the lamb's still roasting!"

The restaurant window bowed under the pressure and a small crack appeared.

Casper mimed for the villagers to move back. "We can't take much more of this!"

"OK, fine." Julius flung a tea towel over his shoulder and smoothed down his thinning hair with the back of a wooden spoon. "How do I look?"

"Erm…"

"Great! Here we go." He strode through the restaurant with an air of royalty, reached the door and flung it wide.

Ting-a-ling.

"I declare The Battered Cod… OPEN!"

Or at least, that's what he would've said. He got as far as the 'de—' of 'declare' before he was crushed by a stampede of idiots.

Instantly, every table was full.

"BEEF!" roared Mayor Rattsbulge. "AND A PIE! WITH BEEF IN IT!"

"I'll 'ave a plate o' yer finest veggibles,"

slurped Sandy Landscape, "with the mud left on. Yummer."

"Hang on!" shouted Casper, dashing to the kitchen for his pad of paper and a stack of menus. "We can only serve what's on the menu. Which of you can read?"

An awkward silence fell on the restaurant.

"Right." Casper climbed up on to a chair to read from the menu. "Everybody listen up and I'll take your orders afterwards."

A deafening *KABOOM* kaboomed from the kitchen like a baboon in a car.

Julius poked his charred head round the corner and grimaced at Casper. "The lamb's… er… sold out."

"OK," – Casper had to improvise for the baying villagers – "some food might take a while.

Bear with us."

"BEAR?" boomed Mayor Rattsbulge. "YOU SERVE BEAR? I'LL TAKE TWO!"

Little Mitch McMassive squeaked, "One pea! Steamed. With a grain of rice for starters." Mitch only had a small appetite.

"Nine saucers of milk!" yelled Mrs Trimble and her cats.

"Do you do jelly beans?" warbled old Betty Woons, who only really ate things that involved jelly beans.

Clemmie Answorth fell off her chair.

In defeat, Casper dashed back into the kitchen with an empty pad. "Just serve what you have, Dad. I don't think they'll remember what they've ordered, anyway."

Soon there was food on every table and odd

brown cocktails filling each glass. The diners ate merrily, stuffing saucy handfuls of nosh into their mouths and tugging on Casper's arms for more. Mayor Rattsbulge had already finished his fish and fish and fish and chips (and the plate they came on, which he'd bolted down with extra ketchup) and was invading other tables for more. Amanda gleefully poured and shook, stirred and blended, but all her cocktails ended up the same muddy colour with that vinegary stink from brown sauce. Not that the villagers minded – they gargled back pints of the stuff or poured it on their food and called for seconds when they'd run dry.

Casper had to admit this was going pretty well. When he carried out the pudding, a great big Victoria sponge iced with a red, white and blue Union Jack, the diners let out a gasp of pure patriotic awe.

"It's a most bootiful fing I've ever did seen," drooled Sandy Landscape.

"Makes me proud to be hungry," boomed Mayor Rattsbulge.

Casper dished out bowlfuls to every table and gave the empty tray to Cuddles, who sat in the basin licking the plates clean. "Dad, look at them all!" he cheered, nudging Julius. "We're a hit!"

"We are?" Julius hadn't given himself a free moment to look out into his restaurant all evening, but when he finally did, his eyes welled up with happy tears. "*We are!*" He threw a gravy-sodden arm round Casper and sniffed, scrunching up his eyes.

"You all right?"

"Just the onions," he sobbed. "They always get me."

Casper knew there weren't any onions, but he had no desire to point it out now. This was a nice moment, he thought. His dad deserved it.

Ting-a-ling.

A gasp fell from the villagers' lips. In the doorway stood Renée, squat and compact, with the little cigarette hanging from his lips. But he wore a brand-new white jacket and a puffy white chef's hat.

"A fluffy white," – Casper gasped – "*chef's* hat."

"ZE FREE OMELETTE!" Renée announced.

"What on earth…" whispered Julius, wiping his eyes.

"Come wiz me, all of you," announced Renée,

stepping back and beckoning to the villagers. "You are not wanting zis, 'ow you say, swill for ze pigs." He turned to Julius, flashed a rotten-toothed smile and spat at the floor. "Free omelette for everyone. She is *délicieux*! Come, come…"

"What d'you mean, free?" squawked Audrey Snugglepuss.

"Free! None of ze money! *Rien!*"

The diners cheered, chairs scraped and suddenly every idiot was making for the exit.

"Stop! Don't go!" shouted Julius, but half of them were already trotting across the square towards Renée's cheese shop. Except that Renée's cheese shop wasn't a cheese shop any more. Casper's tongue went dry as the changes presented themselves. The building glowed radiantly with hundreds of candles inside and out. Crimson velvet curtains lined the windows and a large black sign adorned the entrance with squiggly French writing that read *Bistro D'Escargot*. It was a restaurant. A French restaurant.

"Dad, what's going on?"

Julius was shivering. "Oh, no no no no no." And just like that he was off, chasing after the villagers through the heavily perfumed doors of *Bistro D'Escargot*. Casper followed.

Inside, half of the villagers already had their omelettes. Renée carried two plates through the swing doors from his kitchen, grunting "*Bon appétit,*" as he plonked them at the tables and shuffled back to the kitchen for more.

Then Casper heard it – that hideous wheezing and the wobbly rattle that could only mean one thing. "Lamp!"

The kitchen doors burst open again as Renée emerged with another two plates. Behind him, in an otherwise empty kitchen, were Lamp and the Omelette Gun. One was making omelettes while the other did a highland fling.

"What are you doing?" Casper yelled, pushing through the kitchen doors.

Lamp grinned at his friend. "Renée wanted me to show him my Omlit Gun. He's got loads of eggs too. It's brill!" He cracked three more eggs into the mouthpiece from a huge crate of the things and bounced off again for another dance.

Shouting broke out in the restaurant as Julius started knocking omelettes to the floor.

"Lamp, turn that thing off."

"Why?"

"Just do it, OK?"

Lamp pulled a glum face and tapped '0' into the calculator.

"Right, come with me." Casper dragged him out of the kitchen, finding the restaurant in a state of panic as Julius and Renée wrestled over a plate of omelette.

Casper hadn't a clue what was going on, but there'd be time to understand later. For now, what was needed was action.

"No more omelette!" announced Casper. "Sorry, we're all out."

Disappointed sighs came from the villagers who'd not had one, and from Mayor Rattsbulge, who'd only had six.

"*Non!*" roared Renée. "There is many more of zem!"

But the villagers had got up again and were making their way back to The Battered Cod.

"That's right!" said Julius, running along the cobbles beside them. "Fish and chips, pie and peas – proper English grub."

"Omelette wiz 'erbs!" Renée hadn't given up.

"For free! I give you!"

Many of the villagers turned back.

"Spotted dick and custard!"

"Ze butter, ze eggs, ze beautiful 'erbs!"

The villagers were spinning in circles now.

"FRENCH FOOD IS POISONOUS!"

"ZE ENGLISH FOOD IS BLAND!"

Both chefs tugged at a blubbery arm of Mayor Rattsbulge, trying to gain control of the village's biggest customer. In the middle, the fat mayor was growing ever more angry and ever more stretched. "STOP IT!" he roared. "STOP IT OR I'LL BEHEAD YOU BOTH!"

Julius and Renée dropped the mayor's arms, standing back, embarrassed.

Mayor Rattsbulge smoothed down his robes and took a bite of his emergency sausage. "Now, listen here. I'm all for the idea of eating two dinners," he said through his sausage, looking from one chef to the other, "but this two-restaurant business is taking away valuable dining time. Why, while you stand out here squabbling, I could've stripped bare three racks of ribs. I just won't have it. I won't!" He broke the sausage over his knee, throwing the two pieces to the ground. There were tears in the mayor's eyes. "Now look what you've done. I've gone and lost my appetite! No, this just won't do. There can only be one restaurant in Corne-on-the-Kobb."

"Thank you, Mr Mayor," began Julius, bowing apologetically. "That's exactly what I—"

"We'll have a cook-off. Here in the square on Friday night. We'll all vote, and the chef with the best food wins. The loser must leave the village for good. Simple as that."

The villagers cheered.

"Now, if you'll excuse me, I've got a sausage to eat." And he stomped back to his mayoral lodge (the one with the extra-wide door), wobbling as he went.

Silence fell as the two chefs met each other's stares.

"What are you doing here, Jean-Claude?" Julius demanded.

A broad grin spread on to Renée's face, breaking into a gritty old laugh that shook the ash from his cigarette and the hat from his head.

The villagers started giggling too.

"Dad," rasped Casper, blushing. "He's called Renée."

"*Non*, your fazzer is right." Renée's smile

dropped suddenly. He plucked the stub of his cigarette from his lips with three grubby fingers, tossed it to the cobbles and ground it under his foot. "Renée is not my name, ze cheese shop is not my, 'ow you say, game. I am 'ere to do only one thing – to *ruin you*. On Friday, I will finally be 'aving my revenge. And you," – he prodded a dirty finger on Julius's nose – "you can do nussing. NUSSING. HA!"

The man Casper had known as Renée stormed back to his restaurant. Those villagers who still wanted omelette scuttled after him like pigeons after a gingerbread man, with Lamp galumphing along at the back.

"What a nutcase, eh?" Casper nudged his dad and grinned up at him, but the expression that met his wasn't an amused one. It wasn't even bemused.

It was *de*mused, if anything. Casper had never seen his father's face so white, not even after that time he fell asleep in a bowl of flour. This was bad, and worst of all, Casper had no idea why.

"Come on, then," Julius said, without gusto or interest or even a capital letter at the beginning of his sentence. He shuffled towards The Battered Cod, the already omeletted half of the village following him.

Ting-a-ling.

The rest of the evening's service went by slowly, with Julius wandering about the kitchen in a dream. There wasn't much more to serve, save for jellied eels and some glasses of English rainwater, but even those went down well with the remaining customers.

Once the diners had all dispersed and the doors

had been locked, Casper found his dad slumped face down on Table 4.

"Wasn't that bad, was it?"

"Sit down, Casper."

"Oh. All right." In front of Casper on the table sat a crumpled shoebox marked Tax forms etc. No long-kept secrets hidden in here so there's no point even looking.

"What's in there?" asked Casper, although he probably didn't need to.

Julius looked up. "I think it's time I showed you something. Lift the lid."

So he did.

Chapter 6

The Guilt Box

Outside, the square was dark, but warm light and the sound of the Omelette Gun wafted from *Bistro D'Escargot.*

From the kitchen came much crashing and tinkling as Amanda and Cuddles did the washing-up.

"Be careful, Mum," called Casper.

"What, even with these frisbees?" Amanda

launched a grubby white plate across the room. It whistled past Casper's head and smashed against the far wall.

"Yes," groaned Casper. "Especially with those frisbees." He turned back to his dad and the matter in hand.

Julius's eyes were sullen and far-off. He handed Casper the first yellowed newspaper clipping from his box and motioned for him to read.

Critic hits Britain for Culinary Road Trip

Chefs across the country are quaking in their Beef Wellingtons as renowned Frenchman and food critic Jean-Claude D'Escargot announces he is to tour Britain, searching for "any food zat is not making me sick in my mouth". *He wrote today in his column for Paris newspaper* La Grenouille *that he is to spend two weeks in England to see if its food really is as bad as he's been told.*

"Jean-Claude?" Casper frowned. "But that's the name you called Renée in the square."

Julius nodded. "Now this." He unfolded a long strip of newspaper with paragraphs in French, each separated by a single asterisk.

"What are these?" asked Casper.

"His reviews."

"What about the asterisks?"

"Those are star ratings. He's pretty cruel."

- World of Bacon, Puddleford: *Mal.* *
- Snack Shack, Little Grimston: *Trop mal.* *
- Lady Augusta's Spiffing Coriander Establishment, Upper-Crustenbury: *Dégoûtant!* *
- Donny's Donut Diner 'n' Dental Care, South Grunk: *Terrible! J'ai vomi.* *
- Porridge or Bread or Both, Bittenham: *EUGH! PAH! EUGH! Nourriture pour chiens.* *

"Did that last one mean 'dog food'?"

Julius nodded gravely. "But look." He pointed at the final review. Below the title there were just three words and three stars.

Ze Boiled Sprout, Corne-on-ze-Kobb:
Not zat bad. ***

Casper stared, amazed. "You told me about this. It's your old restaurant. You wanted this review on your gravestone."

"Yeah." Julius nibbled on his lip. "What else d'you notice?"

Casper leant closer. "Well, it's the only review above one star. That's good. And it's in English. The rest's French. So…" Then it hit him. Casper felt his jaw drop. "Oh, Dad, you didn't."

Julius winced and squeezed his eyes shut. "I wrote the review, Casp."

Casper's head spun. "But how?"

"He came on a Saturday night. The place was packed, but he demanded that everyone must leave so he could taste the food properly. He sat down, ordered everything on the menu and said if the starters didn't arrive in five minutes I'd be getting one star. I tried my best, I really did, but he took one sniff at the food and roared insults that made me glad I couldn't speak French. He repainted the walls with my soup, gave me a facemask of spaghetti and poured my blancmange down the toilet. The only thing he did like was the wine. I'd been keeping a couple of bottles of vintage Bordeaux that your granny gave your mother and me as a wedding present. He knocked the first glass back in one, gargled and held out his glass, so I poured another. 'Zis wine, she is like 'ome,' he said, and glugged down more. 'Is good. More.' I poured him another, then another. He sank down in his chair with a blissful smile. I opened the second bottle. In the end he could hardly string a sentence together, let alone pick up his pen. The pad was sitting right there, so I… I helped him along."

"You wrote your own review when he was sozzled?" Casper couldn't hold back a chuckle.

"I only gave myself three stars," Julius said, rubbing his forehead. "Didn't want to give myself away."

"Dad, that's amazing."

"It's cheating, Casp." He rifled through the shoebox again, lifting out a small crumpled newspaper column. "Look what happened."

Top Critic Hounded out of France

Jean-Claude D'Escargot has been forced to flee France after committing the only crime still punishable by guillotine: complimenting an Englishman's food. In his recent tour of England he described one meal as being 'Not zat bad.' His comment sparked violent riots in Paris, resulting in the toppling of the Arc de Triomphe and another revolution. The fact that his review was written in English added insult to injury. The President of France was allegedly on the verge of declaring war on D'Escargot late last night, but decided against it after a steadying glass of Sancerre. On returning to Calais by ferry this morning and finding himself pelted with dynamite-filled croissants at the arrivals lounge, D'Escargot dived headfirst into the harbour and disappeared underwater. There have been no sightings since.

"He deserved it," said Casper.

"I ruined his life, Casp. Nobody deserves that."

Casper noticed his dad's fingers were shaking as he picked out a small cream envelope. "Two weeks later I got this."

Inside, a square of paper held a single word.

Revanche

"You probably think it's nonsense. Or some sort of code." Julius smiled knowingly.

"It's French for 'revenge'," said Casper.

"Well, no. I looked it up. It's French, you see."

Casper sighed.

"It means 'revenge'," his father explained.

"But how long ago did you get that letter?"

"Three years ago," murmured Julius, staring at the wall. "Took me two years to work out the meaning. That word has haunted my dreams every single night since. *Revenge*. I knew he'd come for me eventually. Looks like he finally has."

"But hang on, why didn't you recognise him earlier? I mean, if he's haunted your dreams for years…"

"Well, it seems obvious *now*," Julius snorted. "You'd be surprised what a shave and a change of hat can do to a man. Anyway, I thought all French people looked the same."

"Not all of them, Dad. Only Jean-Claude and Renée, and that's because they're the same person.

Perhaps if you'd noticed that, we wouldn't be in this hole now." With a grimace, Casper put the lid on the shoebox and slid it away from them. "So. What do we do?"

"There's only one thing we can do. We close the restaurant, we pack our suitcases and we leave for Africa."

"Africa? Are you mad?"

"Isn't that far enough? Fine, what's that place with all the penguins? Mexico, that's it. Do the buses go there? We'll start a new life, live in an igloo, eat salted fish. I'll have to take a new name, obviously. I've always liked Rupert. You can be Solomon Junior."

"No way, Dad." Casper shoved his chair back and stood tall over his dad. "We're going nowhere. You've put on a whopping spread tonight and the villagers loved it. What did he do? Omelette. You've got this in the bag, Dad. You're going to win the cook-off on Friday and send Renée packing."

"Jean-Claude."

"Yeah, him."

"Send him packing. Right." There was no strength behind Julius's voice.

A long stiff pause fell on the room. Feeling a bit silly, Casper sat down again.

Julius sighed. "We're doomed."

Ting-a-ling.

Lamp tumbled into the restaurant amidst a cloud of herbs. "Casper, Casper! Renée loved my invention! Did you see? Did you?"

"What did you think you were doing over there?" cried Casper.

"Omlits. I was doing omlits."

"I saw that!" Casper felt let down, betrayed. His best and only friend had been cooking for the enemy, even after Casper had asked him not to. "But why?"

"Renée asked me to show him my Omlit Gun and… I've done something wrong, haven't I? Your face has gone all scrunchy, Casper, and it only does that when I've done something wrong."

Casper softened as he saw confusion rise in Lamp's face. "Listen to me, Lamp, that man's not what he seems. His name's Jean-Claude, not Renée, he lied about the cheese shop, he's out for revenge against my dad and I think he's using you to help him."

"No!" cried Lamp, shocked. "His name's not Renée?" All of a sudden his face blushed plum-red. "But I've been calling him that all this time! How embarrassing."

"That's the least of it. Did he ask you to make that omelette gun?"

"I'm my own man, Casper Candlewacks." Lamp prodded a thumb into his own chest and puffed up proudly. "I make what I like and I like what I make. Except for my automatic pillow plumper. That hurt." He rubbed his head.

"All right. Just keep it that way. If Jean-Claude asks you to invent something, what do you say?"

"No," Lamp nodded determinedly.

"And if he asks for help, what do you say?"

"No."

"Got it. Promise you'll practise that for me?"

"No."

"Is that you doing it now, or—"

"No," said Lamp, and he turned to leave. "No, no, no, no, yes. I mean no."

Ting-a-ling.

"Keep an eye on him, Casp," said Julius. "Jean-Claude doesn't need anyone else on his team."

"You can count on me," smiled Casper. "I'll watch him like a hawk. I was going to keep an eye on him, anyway. There was something weird about him today."

"What, more weird than normal?"

"Way more weird than normal."

Chapter 7

A New Dawn

Like Tuesday mornings tend to do, it arrived soon after the end of Monday night. Casper yawned his way down to breakfast.

In the kitchen, Cuddles was bashing her bowl of mashed banana with a plastic fork while Amanda tried once more to make toast. Her latest attempt (putting bread in the kettle) had produced some soggy results and a terrible pot of tea.

Casper checked the cupboards and pulled down the mouse-nibbled box of Funky Flakez. On turning back round, he found Cuddles wearing a proud little grin and an empty bowl on her head. The mashed banana was dripping down the front of the fridge. Cuddles giggled and stuffed her mouth with thirty-seven pence from the kitchen table.

"Now, come on, darling." Amanda scraped the banana back into the bowl. "Those coins just won't keep you going till lunchtime."

Cuddles jangled and spat out a penny.

"Growing kids like you need all the food groups: fruit, dairy, jelly, bacon, carbohydrates, spaghetti and… erm… help me out here, Casper."

The box of Funky Flakez contained some mouse droppings, the ripped plastic bag and a grumpy mouse, but not a single Flake, Funky or otherwise. Casper put the box back on the shelf. "Mum, leave her. She doesn't like fruit, OK?"

"Ooh, actually," she chirped, "Cuddles does catch a lot of birds. Are they a fruit?"

"Close enough," Casper grimaced.

Cuddles squawked like a seagull and batted the mashed banana away once more.

The second day of school awaited Casper at the other end of a tractor 'n' train carriage journey. He groaned into his empty bowl. What he really needed was a bodyguard – a friend even stronger and fiercer than Bash Brewster. "But that's not going to happen, is it, Cuddles?"

Cuddles was busy grazing the varnish off the kitchen table with her fangs.

"Or *is it*?" Casper's eyes lit up and a plan

hatched inside his head like a sneaky newborn chick with a plan inside its head. "Mum?"

"Hmm?" Amanda was trying to light the bread on the scratchy bit of a matchbox.

"Isn't it time Cuddles started going to school?"

"Oh, is she old enough? What age is normal?"

"Any age, really. She's very bright."

Cuddles bashed her head against the table and grinned at Casper with cross-eyes and a penny stuck up her left nostril.

"Oh. Well, it would be marvellous to get a day off. I like them loads more than days on. Could you take her today? See if she likes it?"

Underneath, Casper's heart pumped manically, but he maintained his composure, not looking up from the plate. "Suppose I could, yeah."

"Oh, thanks, Caspy." Amanda skipped over and kissed him on the forehead. "You're a gent."

This day was getting better more quickly than a jet-plane full of cheetahs in a hurry. With Cuddles, Casper had a first line of defence against the Brewsters. "Come on, girl, let's get you to school." It was tough not to bounce up from his chair and juggle Cuddles down the corridor, but Casper hid his glee, so Amanda wouldn't catch wind of his plan.

Back upstairs, Casper stuffed Cuddles into his

backpack and zipped it closed. Next he searched his cluttered floor for everything else: a dog-eared pad of paper, a cracked biro, a spare yellow tie for Cuddles's uniform and his TuneBrick™, a little music player he'd got last Christmas to drown out Lamp's ramblings. Weighed down with necessaries, he returned to his backpack to find Cuddles standing on top of it, arms held aloft like a champion wrestler, with one foot still caught in the hole she'd gnawed through.

"Cuddles," Casper groaned. "That was my favourite bag." (By 'favourite' he meant 'only'.) Luckily, he had a spare roll of gaffer tape. Unluckily, the bus left in fifteen minutes.

Twelve minutes later, Casper tumbled down the stairs with something resembling a silvery beehive that squirmed and screeched like he'd snared a pair of weasels. "OY! Behave back there or you're not coming," He jiggled his backpack up and down to keep Cuddles quiet.

"See you tonight, Mum!" Casper shouted, slamming the door a bit too hard and taking the doorknob with him. He shrugged and stuffed it in his pocket.

Casper sprinted so fast that all Mrs Trimble saw running past her window was a blur (but then she had lost her glasses). Casper careered down the street, through the park, into the square and on to the train carriage so fast he never noticed Betty Woons soaring about in her new rocket-powered wheelchair, or Mitch McMassive standing on an upturned bucket and reciting poetry to a small but captivated crowd, or Mayor Rattsbulge roaring with joy as he discovered the chemical symbol for sausages. Neither did he notice Jean-Claude sneaking off towards Lamp's garage or even the four new inventions sitting at the doorstep of *Bistro D'Escargot*.

If he had noticed, he would've thought, *How odd...* but he didn't, so he didn't.

Sweating like Mayor Rattsbulge at a pie museum, Casper squeezed down the aisle of the carriage, avoiding the flight paths of paper

aeroplanes and Ted Treadington, and plonked down next to Lamp just as the tractor grumbled into motion, jerking the kids backwards in their seats.

"Hullo, Casper." Lamp barely looked up, furiously scribbling on a piece of paper covered in dense pencil scrawls and a complicated diagram involving an eagle and a garlic crusher.

"What's that?"

"It pipes the choclit sauce into choclit croissants." Lamp chewed his pencil, shook his head determinedly and rubbed out a whole corner of calculations (and the garlic crusher). "I'm putting in a nuclear reactor." He scribbled lots of numbers over the eagle's wings and then, when he ran out of space, drew another wing and scribbled on that.

"Oh." This was wrong. Casper knew Lamp like the back of his own hand (two brown freckles and a scar from the pigeons). His were simple clunky contraptions invented off-the-cuff that took weeks of oily explosions before they finally worked. But now he was messing around with *nuclear reactors*? That was far too clever for Lamp. Wasn't it?

But that wasn't it. More changes struck Casper as he looked about the bus. Across the aisle, Milly and Milly Mollyband, who spent yesterday's bus journey pinching each other, were reciting times tables. Samson Jansen was recreating Botticelli's *The Birth of Venus* with felt tips on the front of his pencil case. But the biggest change, and the only one Casper could explain, was Anemonie Blight. She sat snarling on the back seat with her arms crossed, not doing any bullying at all. In the end, Ted Treadington was so confused that he trotted to the back and handed his lunch money to Anemonie, anyway.

"What's the point?" Anemonie spat. "They'll only nick it once we get there."

"Oh…" whispered Ted, and he put the money back in his pocket.

A muffled snarl distracted Casper from his frowning. Below the seat, his backpack was trying to eat itself.

"Shh," whispered Casper, gripping the backpack a little tighter between his legs.

A light rain pattered on the windows like tiny goblin fingers. Grey concrete buildings lumbered out of the smog and the tractor pulled right off the main road.

"Here we go again."

Casper shuddered to think what role Snivel was playing in his brothers' game of football – if you're interested he was playing the role of goalkeeper's gloves – but he didn't stick around to find out. He fled with Lamp and the other Corne-on-the-Kobb kids, straight through the playground and into school to find the maths room.

"Hey, Candlewacks," smirked Anemonie Blight, plonking her pink bag down on a desk at the back. "Blown up your restaurant yet?"

"Actually, last night went quite well," said Casper proudly.

"Not what I heard." Her pointy nose wrinkled. "I heard you're gonna be driven out of the village cos the Frenchman's a better cook than your daddy."

"He's not!" shouted Casper. "All he does is omelettes!"

"But such lovely omelettes," Milly and Milly Mollyband chimed in together.

"Crispy *and* juicy!" added Ted Treadington.

"Hah!" Anemonie snorted. "Looks like you'd better start packing, Candlewacks."

Casper felt his skin prickle. "How do you know, anyway? I didn't see you at either restaurant last night."

"As if I'd eat your swill." Anemonie turned her nose to the ceiling. "I'm the heir to Blight Manor, not some common serf like you. I'm three-hundredth in line to the throne. I'll get my servants to cook my dinner."

Casper had been to Blight Manor. He knew Anemonie had no servants. The house itself, once the grandest in the Kobb Valley, was now a crumbling rotten heap with half a roof. Nevertheless, Anemonie Blight and her pointy mother thought themselves too important to be seen eating in public. Casper would get no support from her.

"Look, my dad's going nowhere, whether you like it or not," Casper said confidently. "You just wait and see." He wished he could share the confidence of his voice. In truth, he was terrified.

Snivel appeared five minutes later, a bit wobbly, but still in one piece, give or take a few clumps of hair and a tooth that he didn't want, anyway.

Then the maths teacher, Mr Flanty, pranced in. He had a floppy fringe and an orange Hawaiian shirt with palm trees and mongooses on it. He'd also brought a guitar. He popped himself down on a stool at the front of the class and tuned up.

Casper groaned.

Chapter 8

The Best Defence

"Today, boys and girls, Mr Flanty is going to teach you about pi," Mr Flanty cooed, lightly strumming the strings. Mr Flanty was the sort of man who saw a lot of musicals and talked about himself in the third person. "Anybody know what pi is?"

Lamp's hand sprang up like it was trying to escape his shoulder. "Ooh! Ooh!"

"No, you lovable scamp," chuckled Mr Flanty,

"Mr Flanty doesn't mean the type of food."

"But I wasn't going to say that," squeaked Lamp. "It's the mathematical constant defined by—"

"Uh-uh-uh." Mr Flanty held up a silencing finger. "If you don't know, don't guess. Now, who wants to hear Mr Flanty's pi song?"

Not me, thought Casper. He wanted to plan some menus or get started on the spotted dick. He wanted to win over the villagers with his dad's *Best of British* and ensure victory on Friday. He wanted to be free of the bullies whom he knew would burst through that door any moment now. He did not, on balance, want to hear Mr Flanty's pi song.

"Let's rock!" Mr Flanty bobbed up and down on his stool, strummed a jolly G-major chord and

started to sing.

"*Oh, pi's a mathematical constant,*

Not a meaty treat you find in your fridge,

If you give it a bit of work, you'll

Find the area of a circle,

Which is useful when you're building a bridge."

Mr Flanty bowed to Lamp's rapturous applause before starting up again.

"*Sing it with me now! Three point one four one five nine two…*"

Lamp was the only one singing along to the second verse, but then again he was the only person who knew the lyrics. Casper and the others watched in bewildered abandon.

Ten minutes later, Lamp and Mr Flanty were still at it. Casper wondered how long the second verse would go on, and whether he should duck out at lunchtime. Cuddles was starting to get quite restless too, so Casper gave her his pocketed doorknob to gnaw on.

"*Nine three nine three two five one nine—*"

SLAM!

Mr Flanty's squeal was accompanied by the

six-note *twang* of a dropped guitar.

Filling the doorway was Bash Brewster and his burly brothers, Spit, Clobber and Pinchnurse. "Lunch munny."

The kids knew what to do by now. Each pulled out their coins and placed them on the desk ready for collection. Lamp pulled out his final egg.

Bash tromped straight to Casper's desk and grinned his toothless grin. "Lunch munny."

Casper's heart was beating out of his chest. He'd brought defence this time in the shape of his sister Cuddles. But it could go so wrong, and then... Casper shuddered to think of the consequences. He lifted his silvery backpack on to the desk and shakily unzipped it. "It's all in here. Help yourself."

"Oh. Fanks." Bash plunged his hairy hand inside Casper's bag and rifled around. He found something hard and sharp. *"Whassis?"*

What he'd found was one of Cuddles's fangs. What Cuddles's fangs had found was a mid-morning snack. The other three Brewsters heard the splintering crunch before they saw what caused it, but when Bash's face contorted with agony they knew something was wrong. The biggest Brewster's arm withdrew from the backpack with a new addition – a snarling baby in a pink all-in-one and a yellow tie, savage jaws locked round his finger.

"AAAAARGH!" roared Bash, jumping up and down and swinging Cuddles round his head like a lousy yo-yo trick. The other Brewsters blundered around, knocking into desks and walls

as Bash clamped Cuddles between his knees to prise his fingers free. With a hefty tug, he flung his hand upwards and Cuddles soared high across

the classroom, landing in the outstretched arms of
Snivel.

Casper stared at the carnage and gulped.

"RUN!" He dashed towards the door, closely followed by Lamp, grabbing Snivel with Cuddles on his way out.

The three sets of footsteps clacked down the empty corridor. In all the bluster of the Brewster hysteria, nobody saw them leave.

"Think we're safe. Good catch, by the way!" said Casper.

Snivel blushed. "F-fanks."

"Why did we leave?" asked Lamp. "I love that song."

A slam from behind them was followed by a fourth pair of footsteps. The boys spun round in terror, only to see Anemonie Blight rushing towards them.

"Anemonie?" called Casper. "What are you doing?"

"I ain't staying in there, am I?"

"Did they see you leave?"

"What? How do I—"

"THERE THEY IS. GET 'EM!" The brutes emerged from the maths room, snarling like caged beasts.

Casper's insides turned to fondue.

"This w-way!" shouted Snivel, sprinting off down the corridor. With no other option, Casper, Lamp and Anemonie hurried after him.

"Can't believe you let them see you leave!" Casper shouted at Anemonie.

"Shut it, Candlewacks. I ain't giving my lunch money to nobody."

Snivel led the three left, down the stairs. Savage hollers from the corridor above told him that Bash and brethren weren't far behind.

Casper didn't dare to look back.

"Do they want our lunch money?" asked Lamp. "I still don't got none."

"I think they want me," said Casper. "And Cuddles. Or at least our heads on a stick." They ducked through the next door on the right and found themselves in a narrow carpeted corridor with paintings of wrongly coloured lions plastering the walls.

Casper sighed. "I think we've lost them."

"I fink not," rumbled something massive blocking the end of the corridor. Something massive had a face, a gnarled hand and breath that smelt of tuna. Something massive also had a name – Bash Brewster.

The four screamed and turned on their heels, but the other three Brewsters already blocked the way they'd come.

"In here!" yelled Casper, swerving through a heavy-looking door to the right. Snivel veered after him, counted in Lamp and Anemonie and slammed the door behind them. Two fat bolts and a wedged chair later, they were safe.

Casper breathed a sigh of relief and turned to view their hiding place. It was a classroom, probably for history, judging by the tinfoil suits of armour and a fossilised teacher slumped at the desk. To the rear was a shelf densely packed with huge dusty old books bound in faded red cloth from the days before paper. (Until paper was invented by Dermot O'Paper in 1662, books were made of all sorts of things – leaves, wool, maidens or thinly sliced ham. Paper didn't properly catch on until the late 1830s.)

Lamp galumphed to the bookshelf, picked out perhaps the hugest and dustiest volume of all (written on papyrus and not maidens, thank goodness) and flipped it open. "Ooh! Medieval tax records!" He flumped into a beanbag in the corner with a face of pure glee and mouthed the words to himself as he read.

On the other side, Bash, Spit and Clobber were using Pinchnurse as a hollow-skulled battering ram.

As Anemonie settled grumpily in a chair, Casper tossed Cuddles on to the floor and rushed to join Snivel by the door.

"It is going to hold?"

"Sh-should do," trembled Snivel.

"And if not?"

"L-let's not f-fink about it." Snivel perched

on the edge of the nearest chair to the door, squeaking every time the door banged. "S-sorry," he whispered. "I'll g-get used to it in a m-minute."

The bell rang to mark the beginning of the next lesson, but the brutes didn't leave.

"Guess we're having a history lesson, then," sighed Casper.

"Goodee!" cheered Lamp, and he skipped over to a desk at the front.

"I didn't mean it. I think that teacher's been there for as long as those books."

The fossilised teacher creaked upright and cleared his throat.

Anemonie screamed.

"While Victorian Britain saw the birth of steam engines, suspension bridges and the humble Penny Black," the teacher began in an ancient creaky drawl, "by far the age's greatest invention was the London Sewage System."

"Yessssss!" whispered Lamp.

Casper groaned and took a seat, half wishing he'd let the Brewsters take his lunch money after all.

The hammering didn't stop once in the whole hour, but even the iron forehead of Pinchnurse Brewster wasn't breaking through that door. (They make the locks to history rooms extra secure in case the facts try to get out.) Casper screwed up some paper and stuck it in his ears to block out the incessant teaching. Then he fed Cuddles a tinfoil suit of armour to keep her happy and tried to scratch out some menu ideas for Friday on a piece of scrap paper. They wouldn't come, though. At the end of the lesson the bell rang and the fossilised teacher dropped lifeless to his desk once more.

"Well, thank goodness for that."

Lamp chanted, "Thank you very much for the lesson, Mister Sir," and returned to the corner with his book.

"Right." Casper stood up. "Now he's finished we can think of a way to escape. Any ideas?"

Snivel shook his head firmly.

"I'm fine here, thanks."

Lamp turned a page and gasped at a very informative bar chart.

"Anemonie?"

"Can't believe you got us stuck in here, Candlewacks," she snarled hatefully at Casper.

"You chose to follow me."

"I didn't follow you nowhere," she snarled.

"I'm a lone wolf. You probably followed me."
Anemonie stuck out her pointy tongue.

"Whatever." Since Casper had met the
Brewsters, he didn't really see Anemonie as a
threat. Neither did Anemonie, by the look of her
sullen frown and wrinkled nose.

Casper searched the room helplessly. "Cuddles,
you got any ideas?"

Cuddles was too busy barking into a mouse
hole to have ideas.

"Looks like I'm on my own, then."

Casper had just about checked the windows
(both bolted shut) when the bell rang for the next
lesson. Like clockwork, the fossilised teacher
creaked upright again and Lamp danced forward
to his desk. "While Victorian Britain saw the
birth of steam engines, suspension bridges and

the humble Penny Black, by far the age's greatest invention was the London Sewage System."

Casper threw his head in his hands. "You have to be joking."

Lunch came and went, but the brutes' battering ram didn't run out of battery. Casper's stomach rumbled like a runaway wagon and, unlike Cuddles, he'd never developed a taste for tinfoil.

The fossilised teacher delivered his lecture on sewage systems three more times in the afternoon, and each time Lamp sat at the front nodding intently. By four o'clock, Casper was about ready to open the door and let the Brewsters bludgeon his ears off, but then the final bell rang and the fossilised teacher slumped to the desk one final time. The Brewsters instantly forgot what they were doing, cheered "'OME TIME!" and bundled off home for milk and cookies. Once the coast was clear, Casper and Snivel tore Lamp and Cuddles away from books and mouse holes and scampered back to the bus. Anemonie trudged behind.

"D'you want to come back with us?" asked Casper, noticing the worry on Snivel's face. "You can help out at the restaurant, or—"

"It's fine," said Snivel. "There's a l-lock on my b-bedroom door."

"OK," Casper frowned. "See you tomorrow."

Snivel gave a pained smile and padded off.

The journey home was a very subdued affair, but Casper wasn't sure if it was because of the effects of the Brewsters' bullying, Cuddles's afternoon nap or the fact that most of the kids were reading dense philosophical texts. It was the first silence he'd had all day – finally, an opportunity for

another go at Friday's menu. He needed to think up something special; food so tasty it'd blow Jean-Claude out of the water for good. Inspiration didn't come, but Corne-on-the-Kobb did, and when Casper climbed off the train carriage, the paper was still blank.

Lamp hopped down behind Casper and galumphed away across the cobbles.

"Aren't you going to come and help at The Battered Cod?" Casper called after him.

"Can't," shouted Lamp, over his shoulder. "Got inventions to invent." And just like that, Casper was alone.

Jean-Claude sat hunched on the step of his restaurant, smoking a cigarette and kicking at any pigeons that dared to peck too close. He looked up at the sound of Casper's footsteps and hawked

back a noseful of phlegm to chew on.

"'Allo, *boy*. You are looking forward to Friday?" He chuckled and took a long drag on his cigarette.

How could such a small, hunched man make Casper feel so uneasy? "Can't wait," he replied as boldly as he could manage. "Just planning the menu now." Casper waved his piece of paper at Jean-Claude and stuffed it back in his pocket before the Frenchman could notice quite how blank it was. "What are you going to serve? More omelettes?"

"*Oui*." Jean-Claude's gap-toothed smirk made Casper shiver. "Omelette and more."

"Oh, yeah? What else?"

Straight-out asking was a direct tactic and one that Casper didn't expect to work. He was right. "You think I would be telling you? Ha!" The gritty laugh descended into coughing and Jean-

Claude doubled over, clutching his chest. When it passed, he rose, his smirk replaced by a dog's snarl. At standing height he only measured up to Casper's nose. "Leave me alone, *boy*." Jean-Claude prodded Casper's chest. "I have ze… er… business to do."

Casper stood by as the little chef flicked his cigarette to the cobbles and shuffled off away from his restaurant.

"What business is that?" thought Casper as Jean-Claude disappeared round a corner. Perhaps this was a chance to scope out the opposition, have a peek at what Jean-Claude was planning. Without really meaning to, Casper found himself tiptoeing from shadow to shadow, Cuddles jiggling around in his backpack, following Jean-Claude out of the square.

Chapter 9

A Village of Brainiacs

If Jean-Claude had turned round, he probably would have seen Casper following him. For all the leaping between shadows Casper was doing, he was no more invisible than when he walked normally, and Cuddles made squeaking noises every time she hit the roof of his bag. But Casper felt like an action hero, and in the end that's all that matters, isn't it? Anyway, Jean-Claude was so determined to get wherever he was going that even if a herd of elephants with funny hats stood by the side of the road trumpeting the tune to *Dancing Queen* in full harmony, he still wouldn't have turned his head.

The grubby Frenchman shuffled onwards, turning right at the pelican crossing and heading towards Sandy Landscape's allotment by the churchyard. Casper followed (giving the pelican a tickle as he passed), diving behind a hedge to get a good view.

Through a hole in the foliage, Casper could see muddy old Sandy Landscape, just back from his tractor ride, scratching his head at the rows of vegetables.

"'Allo, *Monsieur Landscape*. What is being ze matter?"

Sandy barely looked up. "It's me veggibles. Woke up this mornin' with a few compostin' ideas in me 'ead, so I mixes 'em up and plants me seeds before I goes out on me errands. I comes back just now and, well, 'ave a look fer yerself." Sandy reached down, tugged at some furry green stalks and unearthed a carrot as long, thick and orange as an orang-utan's arm.

Jean-Claude's eyes bulged greedily. He plucked the cigarette from his mouth and flicked it to the ground.

"An' what 'bout these?" An enormous knobbled potato followed the carrot, tomatoes the size of spacehoppers and a fully baked pumpkin pie snipped straight from its stalk. "I's never seen the loike."

Jean-Claude smiled a knowing smile and nodded a knowing head. Then he coughed a knowing cough and lit another cigarette. "Zis is so very... er... unexpected."

"I's better go an' write 'ow I mixed that compost afore I forget. An' that's the queerest bit of all," chuckled Sandy as he lumbered away to his rotting wooden shed, "I couldn't even write afore this mornin'!"

Once he thought he was alone, Jean-Claude let out a chesty chuckle, bringing up a fat flob of black spit. "It works!" he cackled. "*Mon Dieu*, it works!" Unfurling a black bin liner from his pocket, Jean-Claude hastily stuffed the carrot, potato, tomatoes and pie inside, as well as a grubby clutch of fat strawberries from their bush.

"D'you see that, Cuddles? *Thief!*" Casper wanted to leap from behind the hedge and alert Sandy, but already Jean-Claude was shuffling away down the road dragging his bin liner behind him. Who knew what Casper would miss if he blew his cover. He waited thirty seconds and slunk after Jean-Claude once more.

The Frenchman's next stop was the kitchen

window of Audrey Snugglepuss, where a dozen carrot cakes, cut into peculiar shapes, were cooling on the sill.

Casper hid behind a lamppost.

Through the window he could hear Audrey whistling Christmas carols, but when she saw Jean-Claude sniffing at her cakes, she stopped. "Aren't they a picture? I cut them to the shape of my twelve favourite irregular polygons. Look, I even iced in the interior angles."

How odd. Audrey's cakes had come in circles for as long as he'd known her (or ovals if she'd dropped them) – never ever any of this irregular polygon stuff.

Jean-Claude's gasp sounded as fake as Betty Woons's wooden ear. "Zat is quite something, *Madame*."

"I'm just going to check on the next batch. You watch the pigeons don't steal those cakes, will you?"

"Of course," chuckled Jean-Claude, tipping the cakes into his bin liner as soon as Audrey's whistling faded from earshot.

"I can't believe this," Casper whispered. But as his mission continued, things only got odder.

"'Ave a snifter of this whisky, Mister Claude!" squeaked tiny Mitch McMassive, who stood on a step by the door to The Horse and Horse. "Knocked a batch up this afternoon. Sped up the distilling process by piping it through me radiator. Course, it's more complicated'n that, but—"

"*C'est délicieux!*" exclaimed Jean-Claude, sucking up the final few amber drops through his cigarette like a tarry straw.

"You think so?" giggled Mitch. "Well, you'd better try this wine. Brewed it this morning in me teapot."

Jean-Claude reached down to take the glass, knocked it back in one and rested on his haunches as his lips curled into a satisfied smile.

As Mitch scuttled away to fetch the teapot in question, Jean-Claude lugged the crate of wine and the remains of the whisky bottle into his bin liner and scarpered.

The afternoon continued in the same fashion.

Betty Woons was keen to tell Jean-Claude about her new creations – Mexican jumping jelly beans the flavour of fiery chilli that leapt into your mouth and burst whether you liked it or not. When Betty rolled off for a nap, Jean-Claude sneaked into her house and stole a whole bag.

Mrs Trimble had taught her cats to sniff for truffles (both the chocolate and the mushroom kinds) and filled three Tupperware tubs with the things, only to discover she was allergic to Tupperware. Jean-Claude gladly took them off her hands.

Mayor Rattsbulge had perfected a sausage-cloning technique at around lunchtime. By the time Jean-Claude shuffled past the mayor's house, it was so full that sausages were tumbling out of the open window. All he had to do was hold open his bin liner and let them rain down.

Casper watched from behind the statue as Jean-Claude dragged his bulging bin liner through the door of *Bistro D'Escargot*. In one afternoon of scavenging he'd successfully stocked his restaurant without lifting a finger. But more confusing was quite *how* all the villagers had produced their foodstuffs. Sandy Landscape was a terrible gardener – he'd spent most of his adult years planting cornflakes and frozen chips in his allotment. Mitch McMassive had left his last batch of beer to ferment so long that it grew a brain, invaded his pub and only agreed to leave once he'd emptied the till and fed it all his pork scratchings. But here they were, distilling fine whisky in radiators and growing pumpkin pies with special fertiliser.

As Casper trudged home, his stomach grumbled loudly enough to wake Cuddles. Something was wrong and Casper felt sure as beans it was down to Jean-Claude. But what? And when? And whom? And why? And what?

Casper found his mum lying on the kitchen floor, bound from head to foot in a thick tangle of blue wool.

"Hello, darling!" Amanda sang, as if lying in a wool cocoon was the most normal thing to do on a Tuesday afternoon.

"What are you doing down there?"

"Learning to knit. How do I look?"

With a sigh, Casper plonked Cuddles down on the sideboard and set to work on the wool with a pair of kitchen scissors. "At least you gave it a go."

"I was doing a dress, but I forgot the arms. But honestly, who needs arms, anyway? Not me!" she trilled.

"Where are
your knitting
needles?"

"Needles? Ooh, I
knew I'd forgotten something."

Cuddles burped.

"My little schoolgirl!"
squealed Amanda,
clambering free of her dress
and trotting to the sideboard.
"What did they teach you at
school?"

Cuddles yawned and out of
her throat came a strange noise
– a tuneful sort of gargling

in a deep American accent.

"*Ooh yeah, ma darlin', your love is like a garbage truck.*" Cuddles snapped her mouth shut and the noise stopped.

Casper and Amanda stared at the baby, mouths agape.

She giggled and the noise started again. "*Collectin' ma trash on Mondays 'n' Thursdays, doo be doo.*"

"I… know that song," said Casper. "It's on my—" he rummaged around in his backpack, but it was missing. Cuddles had eaten his TuneBrick™.

"*Garbage truck baby, except on bank holidays, garbage truck baby, yeah.*" Cuddles bopped along to the music in her belly, waving her little elbows around with glee.

Amanda's eyes had never been so wide. "My

baby can... sing now?" She broke into a grin. "Casper, that school is amazing!"

Casper grunted. "Amazing," he repeated glumly. It wasn't worth breaking his mum's heart this afternoon, so he'd have to play along with it.

"She can even do the drum noises. Listen!"

Casper sighed. "Double music this afternoon. Must've learnt it then." He couldn't afford a new one, either.

With his mum and his sister boogieing away, Casper pulled on his coat and trudged off to the restaurant. There'd be pans that needed cleaning, fish that needed filleting, and (unless Lamp had *finally* finished inventing that self-peeling parsnip) those parsnips weren't going to peel themselves.

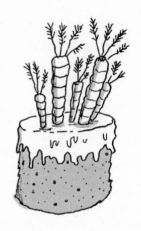

Chapter 10

Humble Pie

After Jean-Claude's escapades that afternoon, Casper wasn't surprised to see that the menu on the blackboard outside *Bistro D'Escargot* had grown since yesterday. Along with *Omelette*, still free for every customer, there was now *Chilli*

Bean Stew, Sausage Soufflé with Whisky-infused Carrots, Pigeon Liver with White Truffle Jus, Potato à l'Escargot and hot *Pumpkin Pie*, followed by *Carrot Cake* or a selection of *pastries* for dessert, each one piped to bursting with gloopy chocolate sauce. There was free seed for the pigeons and a cold meat selection for people who didn't like warm meat.

There were queues outside both restaurants, however, and Julius's menu was, if possible, even more British than yesterday. Casper dashed inside just in time to dole out the first steaming plates of *Haggis and Tartan Sauce, Lancashire Hotpot with Steamed Pound Coins*, extra-messy *Eton Mess* and pots of *Royal Jelly* (made with real royals). All of the courses had been arranged into the shape of Union Jacks to emphasise The Battered Cod's

Britishness, although the *British Beechwood-smoked Rack of Ribs* looked more like a skull and crossbones.

Once the diners had found their tables, Julius led a rousing rendition of the national anthem and waved a big flag. Everybody gladly sang along, but Mayor Rattsbulge replaced the word 'Queen' with 'Mayor' each time it came round.

Amanda skipped in soon afterwards to serve drinks, Cuddles under her arm. The baby's job for the evening was to be a jukebox; Casper stuck Cuddles to the wall with half a roll of masking tape and let the songs from the TuneBrick™ in her belly float through the restaurant, adding much-needed warmth and clinky piano noises.

Casper surveyed the bustling restaurant in awe – the customers were happy. Betty Woons had removed her teeth to suck on a haggis; Clemmie Answorth had fallen off her chair, clutching a stripped-bare pork rib and singing with delight; and Mitch McMassive was smacking his lips with relish as he polished off his breadcrumb. Casper grinned to himself. At this rate, Jean-Claude stood no chance on Friday. Things couldn't get much better.

And then, they didn't.

Ting-a-ling.

Jean-Claude stood in the open doorway with either blood or tomato spattering his chef's whites, arms held out wide as grandly as a stubbly-faced French food critic could manage without not being a stubbly-faced French food critic any more. "Ladies and ze Gentlemans!"

Julius stomped out of the kitchen, his frying

pan held aloft. "OY! What d'you think you're doing here?"

Jean-Claude spat on the carpet and turned away from Julius to the customers. "Zis evening, at *Bistro D'Escargot*, ze Lamp Flannigan lecture series is beginning at last. Tonight—"

"GET OUT!"

"Tonight," continued Jean-Claude, deftly dodging a frying-pan shot, "'Ze Tidal Patterns of North-East Vietnam!'"

Casper looked on, bewildered, as a shiver of excitement passed over the restaurant.

"Ooh!" squealed Audrey Snugglepuss. "Will it be complicated?"

"Oh, so complicate," said Jean-Claude.

"And sums?" added Mrs Trimble. "Will there be sums?"

"Ze sums galore, *Madame*. Follow me!"

Chairs graunched and bottoms lifted, the owners of aforementioned bottoms leaping from their places to follow Jean-Claude.

"No!" screamed Julius. "Are you mad? Who in their right mind wants to hear a lecture about tidal patterns?"

"WE DO!" chorused the villagers, and they piled out of The Battered Cod in an excited heap.

Ting-a-ling.

The sudden silence was shocking. An empty room lay before Casper, save for a stunned Julius standing by the door and a pigeon on Table 4 pecking lightly at a chip.

"Dad, I…" There wasn't really anything to say. He nodded at the pigeon. "At least we still have one customer."

"Would it like a cocktail?" asked Amanda.

Julius just stood there, watching the trail of customers file into *Bistro D'Escargot*.

Casper's stomach growled more loudly than ever. Lamp was delivering lectures now? And the villagers wanted to hear them? And what about this afternoon with all those new discoveries? And the bus journey, where the kids were doing times tables and reading philosophy... What had happened to everybody? It was as if they'd all changed. It was as if Corne-on-the-Kobb was no longer a village of idiots. More like a village of... brainiacs. "Dad, stay there. I'll be right back."

Inspired, Casper dashed out of the restaurant and travelled the length of the square in two twists of a pigeon's neck.

He reached the door of *Bistro D'Escargot*.

"They can't be. Not all of them." He burst through the door shoulder first, like an MI5 agent with a free meal coupon. "Right!"

One hundred sets of cutlery (and one set of Clemmie Answorth) dropped to the floor. The diners gasped and turned to face their invader. Candlelight flickered on each table, casting hundreds of wobbly shadows on the velvet-clad walls. At the far end, Lamp Flannigan stood by a flipchart with a cross-section of a wave covered in dense technical calculations, the drawing of a drowning stick-man and a misfired omelette. He held a long breadstick like a pointer, although there was a bite out of one end where he'd pointed it too close to Mayor Rattsbulge. There was quite a long pause, and then Lamp said, "Hullo, Casper."

Casper's face went all red and he felt a bit silly.

Why the big entrance? "Um, hi."

"What you are wanting, boy?" The challenge came from Jean-Claude D'Escargot, his arms folded sternly and another soggy cigarette flopping from his lips. A pitying laugh burst from within him. "Hah! You have come for to steal my customers?"

Casper's brain ground into motion again as he remembered his task. "No, sir. In fact, I'd like to sing your diners a song."

A raspberry ripple of excitement spread through the restaurant.

"Ooh!" cried Audrey Snugglepuss "Do you do requests?"

"Sing 'God Save our Mayor'!" shouted Mayor Rattsbulge.

Jean-Claude snorted. "What is zis nonsense?"

"I give up, sir. I'm swapping sides. Sinking ship and all that. You're obviously going to win this Friday, so what's the point sticking with my dad? I thought you might want… some entertainment. Y'know, as an apology."

A sparkle of victory crossed Jean-Claude's face. "I am seeing you did not inherit your fazzer's stupidity. You are forgiven, boy." He rested a hairy hand on Casper's shoulder.

Casper shuddered under the Frenchman's grip. "Yeah."

"*Monsieur* Flannigan, do you mind zis interruption?"

"I love songs!" wiggled Lamp, laying aside his breadstick. "Can I do dancing?"

Casper scowled at Lamp. If he let himself say all he wanted to say about breaking promises and batting for the wrong team, he'd give himself away. *Later*, Casper told himself. For now, the time had come to sing. Casper cleared his throat and took a moment to swallow down his nerves.

Jean-Claude leant back against the wall and watched Casper with a thick-lipped smirk.

A hundred pairs of eyes watched Casper expectantly. His knees knocked, his heart fluttered, his hands couldn't find a comfortable place to hang. *Here we go*, Casper thought to himself. *This is it.* Then he felt his mouth open and a noise tumbled out.

"Oh, pi's a mathematical constant,
Not a meaty treat you find in your fridge,
If you give it a bit of work you'll
Find the area of a circle,
Which is useful when you're building a bridge."

Absolute silence. Casper's voice cracked. No point stopping now…

"*Sing it with me now: three point one four one…*"

He trailed off because he didn't know the words to the second verse. But if his theory was correct, the rest of the villagers would know it all too well.

Lamp piped up. "*Five nine two six,*" he sang, "*five three five eight nine seven…*"

Audrey Snugglepuss joined in as well as two bearded women near the front, "*nine three two three eight four,*" smiling at each other as if sharing a private joke. Now half the room was chanting along – even Clemmie Answorth from her heap on the floor. Lamp stood up from his chair, hand clutching his heart, and sang the numbers with gusto. "*SIX TWO SIX FOUR THREE THREE—*"

Casper shuffled backwards. So he was right

after all. The whole room was standing proudly, singing together with delight filling their eyes, fire filling their hearts and the first million digits of pi filling their brains. Everyone, that is, apart from Jean-Claude. He stood cross-armed, his lips curled wryly and his eyes glinting. He turned, flicked the stub of his cigarette at Casper and strolled back into the kitchen with a little wave over his shoulder.

Casper's brain spun. Reeling, he staggered backwards through the door and scrabbled over to The Battered Cod, the sound of chanting filling the square with its eerie tunefulness.

Julius was standing just where Casper had left him. "OK. This is weird."

"What is?"

"The villagers, they've gone all..." Casper

shook his head. It must be some mistake.

"They've gone all *what*?"

At that very moment the crowd burst out into the square in a conga line, each with their hands on the hips of the villager in front.

"They've gone all *clever*, Dad."

"*ONE FIVE ONE ONE SIX OH NINE*," they cheered, kicking out their legs and punching the air.

Julius frowned. "Impossible."

"But there it is," muttered Casper. First Lamp had grown a brain, now the whole village. This was getting weirder and weirder. "That's pi, they're reciting."

"What's pi?" asked Julius.

Ah well, maybe not the *whole* village.

Chapter 10

Rematch

Here are some things you'll always see every Wednesday morning in Corne-on-the-Kobb:

- Mrs Trimble and all her cats in matching white tracksuits jogging muddy circuits of the park
- Sandy Landscape raking up dead leaves to stick back on to the trees

- Mitch McMassive trapped under the beer barrel that he'd been trying to roll inside his pub
- Another of Mayor Rattsbulge's broken beds, left in splintery chunks outside the Mayoral Lodge for the binmen
- Betty Woons feeding grain-flavoured jelly beans to the pigeons

Today was Wednesday. Only a fool or a wrongly printed calendar would deny that, but as Casper made his bewildered way to the bus, he saw quite a different picture from the normal.

- Mrs Trimble and all her cats were jogging on a row of brand-new matching treadmills, built from empty tins of cat food and some long woollen scarves.

• Sandy Landscape was raking dead leaves into the portable compost mulchers built into his pockets.

• Mitch McMassive was effortlessly curling beer barrels across the square, watching them roll to a halt at the pub door with pinpoint accuracy.

• Mayor Rattsbulge was loudly boasting about his new unbreakable bed, reinforced with rods of dark matter.

• Betty Woons was preparing for her wheelchair's first launch to the moon, leaving the pigeons alone to peck at

a plate of omelette left outside *Bistro D'Escargot.*

Casper had given himself the night to think it over, but now he was sure. Somehow, in the last two days, Corne-on-the-Kobb had become a village of brainiacs. The villagers had danced round the square singing 'The Pi Song' long into the night, but nobody had returned to The Battered Cod. He clambered up the steps to the train carriage and sat down next to Lamp without a word.

"Hullo, Casper. Want to know what I'm inventing?"

Casper looked down at the blueprint on the table – no more than a dizzying swarm of pencil lead. "No," he said. Then after a short pause, he added, "You said you'd stop helping Jean-Claude."

"I did, though."

Casper laughed drily. "What about your lecture?"

"But that was for everybody, not just Jean-Claude. Every human deserves to know about North-East Vietnamese tidal patterns, Casper. Don't you think?"

"You drew customers away from The Battered Cod!" cried Casper. "Again! You have to stop doing this. Do you want me to be banished from Corne-on-the-Kobb?"

"No," said Lamp. "I don't want that." Blushing, he pulled a boiled egg from his blazer pocket and poured all his concentration into unpeeling it. "This is the only one today. The hens are being silly."

Whatever was happening to the village, it was happening even more intensely to Lamp. And whatever it was, Casper didn't like it. Lamp's forehead was beaded with sweat, his face furrowed into a frown. He'd glomped the egg down in one and turned back to his invention. But even that was wrong. A week ago, Lamp would never *plan* an invention. He'd just start bolting things together until they went *bing*. "Plans, Casper?" he used to say. "Plans are for people who can spell." Something had changed Lamp and Casper was determined to find out what.

"Casper, will you please stop thinking so loudly?" tutted Lamp. "I'm working."

"Sorry."

Casper let his eyes wander around the bus. It was much quieter even than yesterday. The Mollyband twins, Milly and Milly, were locked in a silent game of chess (and thinking so many moves ahead that neither had started yet).

Eventually, Milly moved a pawn, prompting Milly to smile knowingly and resign. Samson Jansen had filled up the other side of his pencil case with a full piano concerto and now, with a new pencil case, was three-quarters of the way to solving maths.

Anemonie Blight had noticed the change too. "What you doing?" she yelled at Ted Treadington, who had just completed his tenth Rubik's Cube of the morning and stacked it with the others on his table. "Gimme one."

Terrified, Ted passed Anemonie another cube from his bag. "You have to—"

"I know what you have to do, idiot!" yelled Anemonie, gnawing on her lip in concentration. "If you can do it, then I can. It's easy."

Five minutes later Ted had built a scale model

of the Great Pyramid at Giza with his finished cubes, and Anemonie had ripped hers to pieces and sunk deep into her seat in a ferocious grump. She didn't move until they passed through the wrought-iron gates of St Simian's School for Seniors and into its heaving playground.

The first thing Casper saw was little Snivel dashing towards the bus and waving his arms.

"He's happy to see us," said Lamp with a smile.

"Not sure that's a greeting," replied Casper. "Come on." He grabbed his bag of Cuddles and hurried out to meet Snivel.

"G-get back on!" squeaked Snivel. "G-get your d-driver to d-drive away!"

"Why? What's wrong?"

"My b-brothers are after you. Normally they forget but—"

KABOOSH! The big front door of the school slammed back on its hinges as Bash Brewster strode into the playground towards Casper. Bash's right arm was bound in plaster, slung in a sling and thrust in a large pocket on the front of his blazer marked Injerys.

"LUNCH MUNNY!" roared Bash, but Casper was sure he wanted more than that.

"That big boy looks angry, Casper," said Lamp. "Do you think he needs a hug?"

Casper's tongue felt dry. "Stay behind me, Lamp. No hugging anyone unless I tell you."

"Aww."

Spit and Clobber appeared from each side of the large school building, scattering smaller children like skittles in their wake.

By this point Anemonie had jumped off the

carriage behind Casper and Lamp, searching for a quick exit. Sandy Landscape saw the oncoming brute stampede from the top of his tractor, yelped, then drove off in a panic, taking the rest of the class with him. But in the absence of the carriage, Casper could see Pinchnurse striding towards him from the only empty corner of the playground.

Casper's heart sank. "We're surrounded."

"I t-tried to warn you," whispered Snivel.

Anemonie's squinty eyes shifted from place to place. "Candlewacks, please tell me you brought your... *thing*."

"If you mean my sister, then yes. She's here." Casper unzipped his bag and let Cuddles's head pop out.

Bash Brewster let out a yodelling

grunt and stopped in his tracks. The other Brewsters did the same.

"They're sc-scared of her," whispered Snivel.

Cuddles growled at the surrounding brutes, rolling back her lips to reveal two sets of eleven-month-old fangs.

Pinchnurse did a sort of trembling whinny.

"Right, guys, listen up," ordered Casper. "We're safe here while we've got Cuddles, and at least this time we're on open ground. Everyone just stay alert."

So Casper, Lamp, Anemonie and Snivel sat in a circle on the cold tarmac, facing outwards, passing Cuddles round to thrust at any advancing Brewsters. When the bell rang for class, all the other kids trotted inside, but just as before, the Brewsters didn't move.

Casper sighed. "This morning was food tech. Thought I could learn some tricks. The only lesson that'd be any use this week and I'm stuck in the playground."

"Fine by me," snarled Anemonie. "Cooking's for plebs."

"M-maybe your f-friend can teach us fings." Snivel nodded at Lamp. "He seems p-pretty clever."

"It's weird, though," said Casper. "Before Monday, Lamp could barely walk and talk at the same time. Now look at him."

"Hmm?" Lamp's face was buried in a book, while with his free hand he drew out yet another blueprint on a pad of paper balanced on his lap. The book was called *Война и миръ* which was Russian for *War and Peace*, apparently. It had two thousand yellow pages and it smelt mustier than a grandmother.

"How can you invent stuff without even looking?"

Lamp barely glanced at his friend. "It's easy. That's a steam-powered casserole." He grunted and flipped the pad to a blank page, still without looking, and began to scribble again. "Now, a *Crème Brûlée* burner."

"Can we have these for The Battered Cod?"

Lamp shrugged, his attention fully on the book.

"Stop being so brainy," snapped Anemonie. "You're driving me mad."

"Shh, everybody, this is the war bit." Owing to his lack of free fingers, Lamp turned a page with his nose. "It's way better than all the peace stuff."

The thing that disturbed Casper most about Lamp and the villagers' boosted brains was that there seemed no reason for it. Casper thought it over once more as he fed shreds of his geography exercise book to Cuddles. Judging by last night, Jean-Claude had seen the change too; he hadn't looked shocked when they all sang 'The Pi Song'. And then the lecture... Well, Casper couldn't truly blame Lamp for that. If Jean-Claude knew about the brainiacs, then he knew that a dull old lecture would draw the punters in like Sandy Landscape to a spade sale. Casper's cloth-eared friend was innocent to a fault, and he certainly didn't mean any harm. Jean-Claude, however...

Then Cuddles stiffened and gave a demonic screech, ripping Casper from his thoughts.

"What's up?" Casper followed her wide eyes upwards to the overhanging branch of a large oak tree in the corner of the playground. A large tabby cat stared back with gold-flecked eyes. "Oh no."

"TAT!" screamed Cuddles.

"Wh-what's she doing?" Snivel shuddered.

Casper tightened his grip on his feral sister. "She likes cats."

"M-me too."

"TATAT!"

"Not like this, you don't." Cuddles wriggled, but Casper held firm. "As long as the cat stays put, we're fine."

"TATATATATATAT!"

The cat bolted. All of a sudden, things started happening awfully fast indeed…

Cuddles *tore* from Casper's grip like a baby possessed and Snivel DIVED for Cuddles and Cuddles *dodged* and **SCALED** the oak and the cat yowled and Bash's cauliflower ears PRICKED up and Lamp giggled at an amusing turn of phrase and Spit *jumped* and Casper SCREAMED and Clobber **dived** and Anemonie shrieked and Pinchnurse leapt and Lamp *sneezed* and Snivel rolled and Bash BONKED and Casper *ducked* and Spit spat and Bash **BASHED** and Anemonie **dodged** and Clobber got clobbered and Lamp got *dragged* and the book got dropped and Casper found himself *sprinting* towards the school, followed by Lamp and Anemonie and Snivel, with the Brewster brothers in HOT pursuit.

And if you got to the end of that sentence in one breath, CONGRATULATIONS! You and your iron lungs should consider a job in deep-sea diving, didgeridoo playing or pig farming.

"LUNCH MUNNY!" Bash's furious roar echoed down the corridor.

"We've got to hide," said Casper.

"That h-history room," said Snivel. "It's the only p-place we can be sure is safe."

"Yessss!" Lamp did a little skip of glee.

Anemonie groaned.

They veered right, sprinting down another large hallway, and then into the little hallway with all the wrongly coloured lions. There was the history room – decaying teacher still slumped on the desk; everything in place just as before except for the door, which was nowhere to be seen.

"But where's it gone?" Casper couldn't hide the panic in his voice.

"My b-brothers must've t-taken it off its hinges. They're l-learning."

"Oh no," sagged Lamp. "But history's my favourite."

Anemonie screeched. "Look!"

Spit Brewster loomed into the corridor. "Found dem, Bash!"

The four fled again, out of the other end of the lions' corridor and into a small hall lined with doors to classrooms. On one door was painted Art in messy orange letters; on another was a cracked wooden sign with wonky nails in the shape of the word Technology, and a third door simply said Speling.

The stampede was just round the corner now. The nearest door said Caretaker. It would have to do.

"In here." Casper pulled open the door, tugged Lamp inside and let the other two squeeze in behind them.

"Cor," said Lamp. "Whoever Caretaker is, he must be tiny."

The caretaker's room was less of a room, more of a cupboard. Actually, it was less of a cupboard, more of a shelf. The four wriggled for space and Lamp found himself pressed against Anemonie.

"Eurgh, get off me!" Anemonie shrieked, giving Lamp a rough shove.

"Sorry," he mumbled. "There isn't the space not to cuddle."

As three of them cuddled and Anemonie scowled, it was time to take in their stuffy surroundings. The shelf was laden with many multicoloured bottles, a collection of mop heads,

a deflated red balloon and a wonky bike wheel.
But worst of all, *there was no lock on the door.*

Casper gulped. "We can't hide here. They'll find us."

"Ooh, chemicals." Lamp stared at the bottles in awe.

The sound of irate Brewsters filled the corridor. Too late to move now.

"Find dem!" yelled Bash. "I want four lunch munnies an' I want dem now. Or at least by lunchtime."

"Yes, Bash," said Clobber.

"Yes, Bash," said Spit.

"Yes, Bash," said Pinchnurse.

"Yes, Bash," said Clobber, who'd forgotten he'd said it already.

"Yes, Bash," said Lamp, but Casper clapped a

hand over Lamp's mouth and Anemonie thumped him.

There were sounds of stomping and splintering doors.

Snivel trembled like a chipmunk in the fridge.

"Lamp, what are we going to do?" asked Casper. It was hard to stay calm in a room with about three gulps of air left.

"Hang on, Casper, I'm busy." Lamp unscrewed a bottle and sniffed. "Ah, yummy." He nodded, picked up the red balloon and poured a dribble of the liquid in.

This was wasting time they couldn't afford. "If you're not going to help, then come and hold this door."

"But I am helping." He picked up another bottle and read the label. "Ammonia. Mm. Just a drop."

"Ugh, that stinks," gagged Anemonie.

"It's s'posed to stink." He forced a sticky handful of tar down the neck of the balloon, followed by a couple of glugs of floor cleaner. "I'm making a stink bomb."

The Brewsters were getting nearer. In the next room, Casper could hear the sound of overturned tables, overturned chairs and overturned members of Maths Club.

"Anemonie, help us hold this door."

"Shan't." She turned her back on the others (which was silly, given that her face was now pressed to the wall) and made a *hmph* noise.

Bash Brewster's ugly voice hollered from right outside the caretaker's door. "Wot's this one say? C.A.R.E.T… carrots?"

"Th-that's us!" Snivel leant all of his little

shaking body against the door.

Casper's heart raced. "Lamp," he rasped, "quick!"

"Almost there," he hummed, dribbling some liquid from a bottle marked Gin. "You can't hurry science, you know."

"Not even a bit? They're right outside!"

"One final thing," smiled Lamp, fumbling around in his pocket. He pulled out his lunchtime boiled egg and grinned. "Ta-da!" Lamp squeezed the egg down the neck of the balloon, tied the whole thing up and shook it vigorously. Then he grabbed a glue stick and rubbed it on his nose. "You'll all need to glue your nostrils shut. Here."

Casper followed Lamp's lead, plastering it all over his nose, then squeezing his nostrils shut. "Will it work?"

"Course," honked Lamp. "Have I ever let you down?"

"Er…"

Snivel did the same. Anemonie turned up her pointy nose at the glue, plumping instead for a sparkly pink clothes peg she kept in her pocket, mostly for the purposes of pinching people.

Three heavy knocks vibrated through Casper's bones.

"LUNCH MUNNY!" yelled Bash.

"Pretend we're not here," whispered Casper.

"Anybody in there?" called Bash.

"Nope," honked Lamp. "We're not here. Try somewhere else." He grinned at Casper with thumbs up. "What?"

"Shut. Up." Casper mouthed. He bit his tongue, pleading beyond possibility that Bash was dumb enough to fall for Lamp's trick.

There were a few moments of silence. "Oh," Bash mumbled. "Well, fanks, anyway." He plodded off for a few steps and then stopped again. "'Ang on a minute… Dey said… but…"

BAM! Casper and Snivel landed on the opposite wall, feeling the sickening crunch of their bodies before they knew they'd even moved. Bash's silhouette blocked the doorway, ham fists clenched, caveman jowls shaking. Behind him stood Spit, Clobber, Pinchnurse and one nosy member of Maths Club.

Pain coursing through his limbs, Casper crumpled to the floor.

Bash cracked his knuckles. "Lunch Munny."

This was it. Through the pain and the glue, Casper croaked, "Now."

Lamp, clutching his balloon at arm's length like a stinky newborn baby, caught Casper's eye and nodded. With a nasal grunt, he lobbed the balloon through the doorway. It wobbled past Bash's shoulder, floated in the air for a moment and then plummeted to the polished floor in the middle of the Brewsters. All brutish eyes followed the mystery object, watching it strike the floor, watching it burst instantly and squirt its putrid filling into the air like a suicidal doughnut. All brutish bodies jerked backwards as flecks of black porridge-like slime spattered their clothes and skin. All brutish nostrils flared as the foul odour of rotten egg wrapped in a tramp's trousers and left to ripen in a rat-ridden sewer, hit the backs of their throats for the first fetid time. All brutish mouths choked and gagged, all brutish

knees buckled, all brutish eyes watered.

Casper stared at the chaos with a mixture of amusement and horror. With the Brewsters rolling about the floor in a stinky heap, their escape was in sight.

"Ready?" Casper grinned.

They all nodded.

"Then RUN!"

Chapter 11

Deep Cover Dining

"You did it! You actually did it!" Casper leapt into the air, brimming over with triumph. "Thank you, Lamp. I'm starting to like those new brains of yours."

"Boffin…" said Anemonie, who wasn't going to let any saving of lives get in the way of her grumpiness.

Lamp puffed up his chest proudly. "I'd like to

thank my mum, my two ever-supportive hens, and the wonderful world of science." He pulled from his backpack a thick textbook called *Chemistry for Brainiacs (Advanced Version)* and kissed the woman in goggles on the front cover.

"I've had enough of this," spat Anemonie. "You think that was a victory? We just hid in another stupid cupboard and then ran away again. All you wimps ever do is run and hide. I'm doing this on my own. Without you." She stomped off as loudly as she could.

"Bye, Alemony," sang Lamp.

"R-running and h-hiding's all right," said Snivel. "It's w-what I d-do best, really."

"We'll have to do a lot more running if we don't find Cuddles." Casper's eyes scoured the playground, eventually pinpointing a tiny person chewing a book under the oak tree. "Oh, thank goodness."

Cuddles hardly noticed them approach. She was gleefully wolfing down Lamp's copy of *Война и миръ* in chapter-sized mouthfuls.

"My story!" Lamp gazed, heartbroken, at the shreds of paper drooping from Cuddles's chin.

"Sorry, Lamp."

"It's OK." He forced a brave smile.

Cuddles burped (in Russian).

Moments later, the Brewsters emerged from school, ripping at their clothes and rubbing furiously at their stinky skin, but the sticky, tar-based slop clung on like a leech to a blood bank. Staggering at the back was Bash. He'd taken the brunt of the explosion; his entire back half was caked in black sludge, and rubbing it on passing children just made it stinkier. The smell wafting from the four Brewsters was so foul that flowers wilted, insects dropped from the air and a married couple five miles away decided to get a divorce.

The Brewsters stomped off through the gates into town to find a decent car wash without a glance round the playground.

The lunch bell rang and High Kobb kids flooded out of their classrooms. But for all the freedom to cross the playground without being pushed over, to buy lunch without having it snatched from your hands, Casper didn't feel relieved one tiny morsel. He sat on a bench, thinking of all the onions he could be slicing, all the chickens he could be stuffing, if only he was at The Battered Cod. Jean-Claude's meagre Monday offering had grown almost to a full menu by Tuesday. What about today? Would it keep improving? Could Julius even compete by Friday?

At the end of the day, the tractor 'n' carriage rolled through the gates with the Corne-on-the-Kobb kids on board. They all sang Mr Flanty's 'The Pi Song' on the way home, apart from Anemonie, Cuddles and Casper, who blocked their ears, screamed into their blazers or chewed on Lamp's shoe (but not in that order). Casper had a bad feeling about what he'd find in the square on his return, and as the tractor pulled up on the cobbles, his worries were confirmed. A bustling queue reached back from the entrance to *Bistro D'Escargot* to the other end of the square.

Casper leapt off the carriage and dashed over to the villager at the front, who turned out to be

Audrey Snugglepuss; she looked up from her encyclopaedia as he approached.

"Why are you all queuing?" asked Casper. "He doesn't open for hours."

"Haven't you seen the menu? Oh!" she exclaimed, clasping her hands together in adoration. "Just the sound of those dishes stimulates my salivary glands!"

Casper looked at Jean-Claude's Specials board with horror. Just one glance told him all he needed to know. *Caramelised Air with a Bouffant Crust*, it read, *Mute Partridge in Quilted Gravy, Fois Gras Supreme in a Crisped Black Diamond Boat floating on a river of Doe's Tears.*

"What are these things?" gasped Casper, awestruck.

A Figment of Puy Lentils, individually ordained

by the Pope, gently curried in Preserved Saffron Molecules.

Jean-Claude's rubbery little face popped out from the doorway of *Bistro D'Escargot* and smirked at Casper. "*Bravo*, boy. *Encore, encore!*" He clapped his hands sarcastically and Audrey Snugglepuss joined in. "Your little game of singy-song last night was not fooling anybody."

Casper remained steely-faced. "My 'singy-song' told me what I needed to know, thank you very much."

"And what, I may be asking, is zat?"

"The village has gone clever, and somehow it's your doing."

Jean-Claude laughed, his watery eyes full of pity. "Ahh, boy. Why would I be doing zat? What possible gain could I be making?" He hawked and spat black snot at the ground. "Run along home, little one."

"I will!" Casper shouted. "And when I get there, I'm gonna… erm… well… I'm on to you, Jean-Claude!" Purple and cringing, Casper stormed away from the chuckling chef, across the square, through the flock of hopscotch-playing pigeons and into The Battered Cod.

Ting-a-ling.

Julius sat at Table 6 with a mug of cold tea and a frown all over his face. (The cold tea wasn't all over his face, by the way. Just the frown. And a beard.)

"Dad, have you—"

"Seen his new menu?" Julius groaned. "I've seen it all right. *Gold-leafed doodaahs* and *Deep-Cleansed whatnots*. How am I s'posed to compete, Casp?"

"Don't say that. I know you'll win on Friday. After all, the villagers are scared of foreigners. Remember the time they locked that Spaniard in the clock tower? And the Japanese tourists that they tried to make into soup? They're bound to tire of him soon."

"But his food's getting better every day. How's he doing it?"

Casper rubbed his eyes. "I don't know, Dad. I wish I did."

"I need you to go in there. Find out more about Jean-Claude's cooking."

Casper laughed. "I can't just waltz into *Bistro D'Escargot* and ask for his secrets!"

"Why not?"

"Well, d'you think he'd tell the son of his arch-rival? He'd kick me out before I'd even ordered starters."

"All right, clever-clogs. Got a better plan?"

"I need a disguise. I need to look like, well, not me."

"Not you, eh…" Julius scratched his beard. "I've got just the thing."

"I look like a prat." Casper stood in front of the mirror in his mum's yellow dress with frilly sleeves and a plunged neckline along with six-inch scarlet stilettos and pink leggings, topped off with a wide-brimmed straw hat to cover his blushing face.

"What are you talking about?" said Julius. "The colour matches your eyes!"

"As if you know anything about fashion."

"Excuse me! I was something of an icon back in the seventies. Pink bell-bottoms, glittery silk shirts… they called me 'Disco Inferno'."

"I think you've just proved my point."

"You ask your mother. When I stepped on to that dance floor, the crowd would part at my feet."

"Scared of your bell-bottoms?"

"You haven't a clue, Casper. I've still got them somewhere…"

"Talking of Mum, do you think she'll mind? About this dress, I mean."

"Hey, what she can't see won't hurt her."

Casper and Julius had sneaked past Amanda on the way upstairs. She was down in the kitchen, picking scraps of *Война и миръ* out of Cuddles's hair. That left Casper and Julius free to root around in her wardrobe for pretty dresses.

"If you ever tell anyone..."

"I promise, Casper." Julius masked a chuckle by coughing into his hand. "Blimey, if you find out Jean-Claude's secret, *I'll* wear that dress."

"Can't believe I'm doing this." Casper groaned. "I actually look like a girl."

"A rather ravishing one, if I may say so," chuckled Julius. "Just remember to talk like a girl too."

Walking with heels was a lot harder than Casper had expected. Halfway down the stairs, he turned an ankle, missed the step and tumbled the rest of the way, landing in a technicolour heap on the floor.

"Boys! Boys! Over here!" Amanda cried down the corridor. "Cuddles has learnt Russian!"

"Another time, dear. We've... erm... got to rescue the dumplings. Left the oven on." Julius slapped the side of his head, tutted at himself and bundled Casper out of the front door under his jacket.

It was practically dark when they left the house. How many hours had passed since Casper started changing? Many hundreds, thousands, or probably about four if Casper actually thought about it. So many needless frills, so many bits to tuck and fold and glue in place. Casper felt like a Christmas present.

The walk to The Battered Cod was a painful

sequence of falling, climbing up, tottering and falling again. On the upside, at least he was starting to get used to it (the falling, that is, not the tottering – that was still as hard as ever).

The queue outside *Bistro D'Escargot* had disappeared and the restaurant was practically full already, but what with this afternoon's dressing-up session, The Battered Cod was still dark and locked up.

"This better work," growled Julius.

"Just get the restaurant ready for eight.

Remember what to do?"

Julius nodded and looked at his watch. "I'll be there."

"And you're sure you can't tell it's me?"

"Positive, Casp."

"Promise?"

"Promise."

"Promise you promise?"

"I wouldn't recognise you in a million years. Now, go on – get on with it."

"All right. I'm ready." Casper tipped his hat at Julius and trotted into the square, bumping straight into Lamp.

"Hi, Casper. Nice dress."

So much for a million years. "Ahem," Casper squeaked. "Casper? Who's Casper?"

"You are. What's wrong with your voice?"

"Oh no, but my name's… er… Elizabeth. You must have the wrong person. Good day." Casper pulled his hat down over his face and trotted away, tripped straight over a cobble and clattered to the floor.

"Casper, are you OK?"

This was ridiculous. Casper clambered back upright using a wall for balance. He tugged Lamp to a corner of the square and hissed, "Look, I'm undercover and you're ruining it. I'm pretending to be a lady, so I'd appreciate it if you stopped using my name."

Lamp frowned. "But why would you want to be a lady?"

"I'm infiltrating *Bistro D'Escargot.*"

Lamp looked horrified.

"Stop that. It's for my dad. Just pretend I'm

your mum or something."

"Oh, that's easy. I'm good at pretending. Hello, Mum; you're my mum. See?"

Casper sighed. "Good, now take my arm and let's go in."

Lamp obliged, giggling under his breath.

Muddy old Sandy Landscape stood outside *Bistro D'Escargot*, prodding the potted plants by the entrance.

"Hello, Mister Landscape," chirruped Lamp, "have you met my mum?"

"Ooh, er... no... ohh!" He glanced at Casper and instantly fell in love. "I don't believe I've 'ad the pleasure, me darlin'." Sandy leant forward to kiss Casper's hand.

Casper curtseyed. "Much obliged."

Sandy hawked into a hanky. "Will you... er...

be dinin' tonight? After I finished taxonomisin' these ferns, I'll be right in."

"She's my mum, you see," said Lamp, "because it's true."

Casper curtseyed again and tugged Lamp inside, where the garlic-scented villain himself, Jean-Claude D'Escargot, waited by the door.

"*Bonsoir, Monsieur Flannigan.*" His bow brought him out in a coughing fit.

"Hullo, Mister Snail. I've brought my mum," nodded Lamp, "because she's my mum, and I'm me. That's both of us, including my mum, of course."

Jean-Claude dragged impatiently on his cigarette. "*Alors*, if you follow me, zis table, she is for two."

He beckoned the boys through the restaurant;

each table was stuffed with hungry geniuses, gabbling incomprehensibly about quadratic equations or the philosophy of Aristotle. By the look of it, the whole village had got even cleverer since yesterday. Mayor Rattsbulge was always too lazy to use a knife and fork, but now he'd invented a solution – a robotic arm attached to his mayor hat that shovelled food into his mouth. Clemmie Answorth had a battery pack strapped round her body that would harness the energy produced in falling off her chair to keep the food warm. Betty Woons, at the age of 107, had developed enough mental power to bend spoons, much to the irritation of the villagers on the surrounding tables, who were now unable to eat their puddings.

The food itself was a wonder to behold – plates of whizzing, crackling, floating delights, the colours and smells bombarding Casper's nostrils like yummy fireworks. At this rate, Julius couldn't even compete come Friday. Casper knew he had to get inside Jean-Claude's kitchen to see how it was done.

Jean-Claude stopped at a small table in the far corner and pulled back a chair for Casper. "*Madame*," he growled.

Casper nodded, averting his eyes.

While Lamp pored eagerly over the menu, oohing and aahing at every item, Casper pulled the straw hat further down over his head and retreated into his corner.

Moments later Jean-Claude was back with two plates full of yellow stuff. "Your *apéritif, madame et monsieur*."

"Yippee!" Lamp jiggled in his chair.

"Oh!" Casper's squeak cracked so he pretended to do a lady-sized sneeze. "But we didn't order this."

Jean-Claude lips curled at the edges. "My special omelette wiz special *'erbs de Provence*, she is free. For everyone." He waved his arm across the room revealing sweat patches under his jacket. Casper noticed similar plates on almost every table.

Jean-Claude shuffled off, leaving the boys in peace.

"Lamp," Casper rasped, "why's he still got your omelette gun?"

"I don't need it back," shrugged Lamp, "not when Mavis and Bessie aren't laying any eggs."

This was ridiculous. "But you're helping him! *Again!*"

"I'm not cooking them for him. If he wants

omlits he's got to shoot them. And if you don't want yours, I'll have it," said Lamp, tucking into a forkful of his omelette. "Ich ruvvry."

I can't win, Casper thought. *Not without locking Lamp in my basement or something. The problem's with the scheming Jean-Claude, not him.* He inspected his omelette with a fork. It did look delicious – steaming hot, flecked with fresh herbs and black pepper, with a beautifully light aroma that drew his nose closer to the plate. *No, Casper,* his mind scorned, *you're supposed to be spying, not eating. Just get on with the job.* He shook his gaze free and tried to ignore the omelette, but a moment later his attention was drawn once again towards the plate. *Just one bite – surely that can't do any harm? And it does smell so blooming gorgeous. Let's see what all the fuss is about.* Casper's fork hovered over a crispy corner and then cut through its soft flesh, releasing a rich dribble of juice on to the plate. He lifted the forkful, floating it temptingly before his eyes. His mouth salivated as it drew closer. The intoxicating scent flooded his nostrils. This was it. Casper closed his eyes to receive the mouthful, parted his lips, and...

SPLAT!

Casper's teeth clashed on empty air.

What? Where'd it gone? Casper snapped open his eyes and gasped as if waking from a bad dream. Judging by the omelette dripping down the front of his dress and the horribly bent fork in his hand, Betty Woons had moved on from bending spoons.

"What was I doing?" he whispered, inspecting his hand as if it was someone else's. "This food..."

Lamp slurped noisily and swapped his empty

plate with Casper's, digging into the second omelette with relish (tomato relish).

Just on cue, or about thirty seconds after cue if you're going to split hairs, Julius trampled through the front door. His eyes locked with Casper's for a second, but they flicked away as if he hadn't seen him.

"Free books!" he shouted. "Free textbooks with every meal at The Battered Cod!"

The villagers squealed with excitement and rose from their chairs, very much used to this coming and going by now.

"That's right," Julius said encouragingly. "Thick books, long books, not a picture in sight."

"Ooh, that's my favourite!" shrieked Clemmie Answorth, launching at Julius, missing and toppling over a chair.

Julius disappeared out of the door and the villagers pursued, breathless at the prospect of free books. Lamp moved to follow, but Casper grabbed hold of his sleeve and tugged him back.

"Hey!" Lamp moaned. "What about my book?"

"There is no book," whispered Casper. "Anyway, I need you."

"Ze pig, he is lying!" roared Jean-Claude, charging out after the villagers, his stubby fingers waving. "Stay wiz me! We can do ze sums!" The door slammed behind him and the boys were alone in the restaurant.

"Perfect," said Casper. "Now, where's the kitchen?"

Chapter 12

Molecular Gastronomy

Lit by stark white strip lights, Jean-Claude's kitchen was stacked with high-tech cooking machines that whirred and popped with activity, piping out soup or layering pastry with fruit and cream using long, skeletal robot arms. In the corner, Lamp's omelette gun had finished its work, a pile of herby omelettes slipping down the opposite wall.

"Just look at all this stuff!" gasped Casper. "They're the sort of things you'd invent."

"That's not a surprise," grinned Lamp. "I *did* invent them."

Casper felt like his head had been dunked underwater. He spun round to face Lamp, eyes wide. "*What?*"

"*I* invented them, didn't I. That's my *Brûlée* Burner," Lamp said proudly, pointing at a snare drum fitted with six inward-facing blowtorches. "Made that this afternoon. And next to it is my dishwasher." A wooden hutch contained three hungry-looking guinea pigs, licking at one of the dozen or so plates slowly moving along a conveyor belt. "Aren't you proud of me, Casper?"

All Casper could manage was a breathy

splutter. Of all the things Lamp had done to help Jean-Claude, this was the absolute worst. This was *treason*. This was *heresy*. This was double-crossing of the first degree. How could Lamp stand there grinning like a cosy imp when he'd just served Jean-Claude victory on a plate? "How… how *could you*?"

"How could I what?"

"You've sided with him again and again, and now I find this? *You've invented Jean-Claude a whole automatic kitchen!*"

"I haven't!"

Casper laughed bitterly. "Look around yourself and say that again."

"What, these?" Lamp giggled. "I didn't invent them for Jean-Claude. He just gave me the ideas. 'Ooh, Lamp, I bet you can't invent a omlit maker,' he said to me." Lamp's French accent was just a normal accent, but with his head wiggling about. "'I bet you can't build a machine to pipe the choclit into pastries.' Well, I'm not one to turn down a challenge, Casper."

Bile filled Casper's throat. His head throbbed. He took off his hat and scratched his sweating scalp. "He's tricked you, Lamp. Don't you see what you've done?"

"Ooh," Lamp clapped. "Have I won?"

"No. But Jean-Claude has."

"Is that bad?"

"It means I have to leave Corne-on-the-Kobb on Friday. So, yeah. Bad."

Lamp sucked his lip. To draw attention away from the awkward pause, he opened the fridge. "Cor, Casper, look at all this!"

The most exquisite array of gourmet foods lined the fridge shelves, from asparagus tips to juicy pomegranates, Audrey Snugglepuss's cakes, a stack of pretty green bottles marked Lager McMassive and many, many, many, many eggs. In fact, half the fridge was taken up with the little yellow fellows.

"Ooh!" squealed Lamp, stuffing a couple of the eggs into his boiler-suit pocket. "Save them for later."

Casper recognised half of the stuff in Jean-Claude's fridge from yesterday's bin-bag run. "Lamp, it's not just you Jean-Claude's using. It's everyone. The combination of the whole village's cleverness has stocked this kitchen – your machines, Sandy's vegetables, Betty's jelly beans…"

"'Allo, boy."

Casper screamed, wheeled round and found himself face to grizzled face with Jean-Claude D'Escargot.

The dress without the hat wasn't enough to disguise Casper. He'd been foiled. "Ah. Hi. I can explain."

"Zere will be being no need." Jean-Claude clamped his grubby fingers round Casper's ear and twisted.

"AACK!" He tried to wheel free, but the chef twisted harder.

"And you too?" He snatched a clump of Lamp's hair, prompting a million squeals from Lamp's tame nits. "I thought you were better zan zat. Ah well, you have helped me enough already. Come wiz me."

Casper didn't have much choice. If he didn't care so much about his ear, he could have broken away without it, but he'd grown quite attached to the little thing over the years and his other ear would get terribly lonely without it.

So Jean-Claude tugged Casper's ear and Lamp's hair through a door at the back of the kitchen and the boys followed reluctantly, down a flight of crooked stairs, through a thick hardwood doorway and into a pitch-dark cellar. The wind shot out of Casper's lungs as he clattered to the stone floor. Lamp soared past Casper's head and made very good friends with a wall at the other end of the cellar.

"You LOSE!" Jean-Claude bellowed from the doorway. "You lose and I win! On ze Friday, Julius, he is ruined. And you," – he broke into a dirty, tobacco-blackened laugh – "you cannot do nussing. HA HA HA H—"

"Actually, that's a double negative," interrupted Lamp, clambering to a sitting position. "What you meant was we can't do *anything*."

"SHUT UP, SHUT UP!" The door slammed, the lock clunked shut and Jean-Claude thumped

250

back up the stairs.

Casper let his head sag. "Mission accomplished?" he murmured. "Not even close."

"Are we in heaven?" muttered Lamp.

"What?" said Casper, annoyed. "No, we're in a cellar. Just give it a rest."

"No, we must be in heaven. Look around you!"

Casper really didn't want to lift his eyes. But he did so, if a little doubtfully, and there they were. Stacked high on every surface, covering every shelf and piled high in every corner, were hundreds and hundreds of fresh spotty eggs. More than in the fridge – way more. "Why?" Casper's mind spun furiously, but no answers popped out.

"To make omelettes!" cheered Lamp, licking his lips. "One thousand, three hundred and seventy-eight of them, if I've counted correctly, which I have, because I just counted again to check. Well, at least we won't go hungry."

"But why so many?"

"You can't make an omelette without breaking some eggs," Lamp chanted. "And anyway, Jean-Claude has to make bazillions of omelettes. It's his special starter, isn't it."

"Still strange, though. They aren't even in egg boxes – just sitting there on the shelf."

"Maybe he used the egg boxes to make a castle," said Lamp. "I always do that. But not any more because Mavis and Bessie don't lay eggs in boxes like the chickens at the shop must do. Phew." Lamp collapsed on to the floor. "Tell you what, Casper, pretending you're my mum works up quite an appetite. Lucky there's eggs."

Casper grimaced. "I hope there's more than just eggs."

A quick sweep of the room told Casper what else there was to eat – a cardboard box with a tap that had the words House Red Wine. Muck – for customers only scrawled on its side, six tins of peaches (the sort with ring pulls, luckily) and a nervous woodlouse.

"PAH!" Casper coughed a mouthful of wine back out on to the floor. "It tastes off! How can people drink that?"

"My real mum says wine's made of grapes and Jesus. That's why they drink it at church."

"Well, grapes and Jesus taste horrible." Casper put the wine back in the corner and opened a tin of peaches. The boys sat cross-legged in the middle of the floor, Casper drinking peach syrup from the tin, Lamp slurping noisily on his finger and then dunking it back in an egg.

"This is fun," said Lamp. "It's like camping, but we don't even need a tent."

"Bed time, then," said Casper.

"I forgot my sleeping bag," said Lamp. "I'll just pop home and… Oh."

"No sleeping bags this time." Casper patted Lamp's back.

"And I need a wee."

"You'll have to wait until we go home."

"When can we go home?"

"I don't know. Guess we'll have to wait and see what happens tomorrow."

Chapter 13

What Happens Tomorrow

Nothing.

Chapter 13b

What Happens the Next Day

"Morning, Casper," yawned Lamp.

"Is it?" Casper's head throbbed when he opened his eyes, so he closed them again. The cellar light had stayed on since Jean-Claude left and with no window, it was impossible to keep track of time.

"Well, it's breakfast time, and breakfast happens in the morning, so it must be morning."

"If you say so." Casper had hardly slept last night, much like the night before. This dress made his skin all itchy, he was desperate for the toilet and his mind just couldn't switch off. He lay there, wide awake, watching the ceiling, alert as a full-time coffee taster. All the time Casper was imprisoned in this cellar, Jean-Claude was carrying out his evil plans, whatever they were, and he couldn't do a thing. He'd also remembered in the night about Teresa Louncher, who was most likely still stuck in that locker at school. *Not that we're any better off than her*, he thought.

"I really need a wee." Lamp rose from his sleeping corner with bleary eyes and hair like a sooty porcupine. "What's for breakfast, then?"

"Eggs or peaches, peaches or eggs. It's all we've got."

Lamp grabbed two eggs with a sigh and cracked one open on his knee. The first he slurped down in one, and the second he licked slowly like an ice cream.

If Casper had anything in that cellar, it was time. Time and eggs. But mostly time. And in that time he'd rolled the facts over and over in his head so many times, they'd jumbled up like Julius's sock-and-batteries drawer. There were Frenchmen and brainiacs and omelettes and Brewsters, restaurants and stink bombs and egg piles and roosters. (That last one's not strictly true, but 'hens' doesn't rhyme with 'Brewsters'.)

The question remained – why had everyone suddenly added the word 'million' to the end of their IQ? Surely it wasn't a coincidence? The chance of a whole village of idiots suddenly turning into geniuses was about as likely as winning the lottery while getting hit by an asteroid and a bolt of lightning and being swept into the air by a freak tornado, flying once round the world on the back of a talking cow and landing in your bed with a cowboy hat on.

But the mere fact of the village getting brainier didn't bother Casper in itself. What worried him was what the villagers' new brains were being used for. The food they grew, the drinks they brewed, the machines they built... Jean-Claude was reaping the benefits. And that was the thing that kept Casper wide awake long into what he guessed was the night. However he looked at it, this whole mess came tumbling back to Jean-Claude D'Escargot. Whatever was going on, the grubby little Frenchman couldn't *not* be involved.

But that's the point where Casper had each time hit a brick wall. Jean-Claude was a world-class culinary critic; he lived, breathed and (most importantly) ate food. He'd drunk every wine in the Loire Valley and could identify any cheese from six hundred paces. So why would a man of such status go to the effort of turning a whole village into brainiacs, wait for them to make food-related discoveries, poach the results and palm them off as his own? Unless…

"No…" Casper chuckled to himself, "don't be an idiot."

"I wasn't!" Lamp was crushing eggshells together in an effort to make a black hole.

"It'd be ridiculous, but…" Casper jumped to his feet. "It makes perfect sense!"

Lamp tossed his eggshells over one shoulder,

his interest finally sparked. "What are you on about, Casper?"

"Seems so obvious now… *Jean-Claude can't cook!*"

Lamp snorted. "Don't be silly. I've eaten his food. It's good. Speshally the omlits."

"But those are *your* omelettes, Lamp, from *your* omelette gun."

"Are they?" Lamp squinted. "Oh yeah. But he serves loads of other things. French fries and croissants, and this red stuff with chunky bits."

"But those are all made with your machines! With food stolen from the villagers. Didn't you see his kitchen? I'll bet Jean-Claude's never picked up a knife in his life."

"But if he can't cook, then why's he starting a restaurant?"

"For revenge against my dad, Lamp. But he can't do it by himself. You see, Jean-Claude's spent his entire life criticising other people's food, without taking one moment to learn how hard it really is to actually cook it. And that's where you come in."

Lamp looked at the door. "But I'm already here."

"No, I mean… how can I put this?" Casper was, both literally and figuratively, treading on eggshells here. "How often do you normally know the answer to a question?"

"I don't know the answer to that question," said Lamp.

"Right, well, it's not very often."

"Ooh, I knew that!" Lamp cried, slapping his thigh.

"But then, more recently, you've known everything. And I mean *everything*. 'The Pi Song', tidal patterns in Vietnam, how to read Russian, for goodness' sake. All that boring knowledge isn't really yours."

Lamp frowned and tapped his head like a squirrel taps a nut. "Well, then, how did it get here?"

"This'll sound mad, Lamp, and I'm sorry," Casper continued, "but I think Jean-Claude's planted it there. I don't know how he's done it, but you've changed. You and everyone else in this village."

"Not you, though."

"No, not me. And not my family or Anemonie Blight, either. Whatever Jean-Claude's done, it hasn't worked on us. But why are we different?

What marks us out from the rest of the village?"

As he racked his brain, Casper's mind touched on something Anemonie had said in the classroom, her eyes squinting scornfully. *As if I'd eat your swill… I'll get my servants to cook my dinner.* Casper gasped, "That's right! Anemonie never ate at *Bistro D'Escargot*. I almost did, but the omelette never touched my lips, and Mum, Dad and Cuddles definitely haven't. We're the only ones who haven't eaten Jean-Claude's food!" Casper clapped his hands victoriously. "So that's what's making you clever! His food!"

"But, but" – Lamp scratched his head furiously – "you're wrong."

"Sorry, Lamp, I'm not." Casper was excited now, pacing round the room on the tips of his toes. "The food has made you clever and now you're inventing at five times your normal speed. Jean-Claude tricked you and now he's got your inventions. Same goes for all the villagers; all they needed to do was to eat his food on Monday, and they did."

Lamp's face was squished and red. "No, I mean you're wrong. The restaurant opened on Monday night, yes, but geography was Monday morning. I'd not eaten none of Jean-Claude's food, but I still got full marks, remember?"

"Oh…" Lamp's logic felt like a punch to the stomach.

"Maybe my brain just grew. My mum said I was a late bloomer, but I didn't understand because that's about flowers. Now I get what she meant."

"But you're not a brainiac! You can't be."

Lamp's face dropped.

"Oh no, I didn't mean—"

"It's OK. I'm stupid." He turned to face the wall and mumbled, "Three hundred and sixty-seven bricks."

"Lamp, you know I don't mean that. There's just a difference between being a brainiac and being a genius. You're a genius, Lamp. All your inventions, they shouldn't work by normal logic – sometimes they shouldn't even work by *your* logic – and yet they still do. Nobody else could create them but you. But this brainy stuff, that's new. That's *not you*." Casper wished the air were less stuffy, that his dress would stop itching, so that just for one second he could think straight. "We need to get out of here."

Lamp shook his head. "Not possible. The door's locked."

The boys sat down.

Lamp had an egg.

Lamp had another egg.

Lamp had another egg.

Lamp wet himself.

Hours passed.

Casper searched the walls for loose bricks, but he only found tight ones.

Lamp tried to prise the door open with a hydraulic jack made of wine bottles and frothed egg white, but that just ended up with a big puddle of wine and a sticky door. "It's no use," huffed Lamp, "we'll just have to save the day first and escape later.

There was a knock at the door.

Lamp screamed.

"Someone in there?" shouted a muffled voice.

"Yes! I'm Casper Candlewacks and the screaming one is Lamp Flannigan." Casper could feel his voice shaking. "Who's that?"

"Casp? It's Dad."

"Dad!" A rush of excitement spread through Casper's bones. "He's come to save us!"

"Can I come in?"

"I really hope so. It's locked on our side."

The bolt clicked, the door creaked open and Julius's face appeared from behind it. "Casper! Oh, thank goodness, you're OK."

Casper rushed forward to hug his dad, something he saved only for special occasions (mainly because Julius only showered before special occasions). "Thought you'd never come. I thought we were stuck down here, Dad."

"I've been looking all over for you," he grinned,

the relief etched on his face. "I was beginning to think Jean-Claude had cooked you or something."

Casper laughed and gave his dad another hug. "Still raw, thank goodness. What kept you?"

Julius's face went stony. "Jean-Claude's got me beaten and he knows it. Last night he served food so good the customers wouldn't leave. He's been protecting his kitchen in advance of this evening.

"Then, how'd you get down here?"

"Well, he's gone now."

"Gone where?"

Julius tutted. "Don't ask silly questions. Come on, there's no time." And with that he was already trotting back up the creaky wooden stairs.

Uh-oh. There was that rumbly feeling again. It had only been breakfast a minute ago. Why was there no time?

"Can I bring some eggs for the journey?" asked Lamp, looking around hungrily.

Casper yanked Lamp by the arm and dragged him moaning out of the room, not one shaving of an amoeba sorry to be leaving.

"You're not going to like this..." Julius was already upstairs in Jean-Claude's kitchen, but Casper and Lamp were hot on his heels.

"All the machines? Yeah, we've seen th— Oh." Casper's mouth dried up. The machines were, in many ways, not there any more. What replaced them was perhaps more terrifying – eggs. *More* eggs. There were eggs on the floor, eggs on every shelf, eggs filling the basin and eggs caught in spiders' webs in dusty corners. There were more eggs in that kitchen than the entire prized egg collection of Egbert Von Egglestein, a

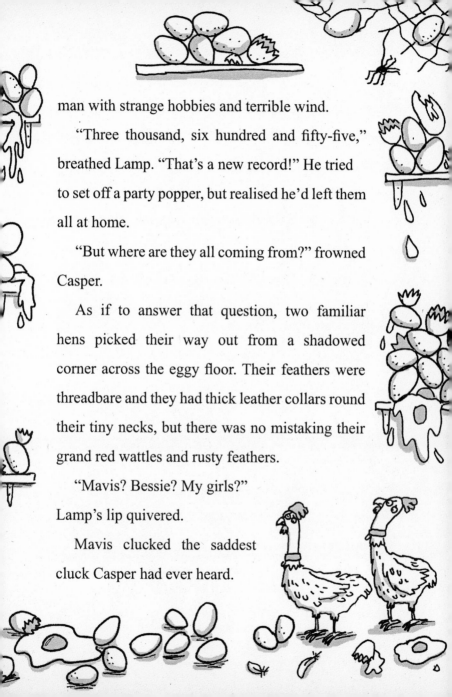

man with strange hobbies and terrible wind.

"Three thousand, six hundred and fifty-five," breathed Lamp. "That's a new record!" He tried to set off a party popper, but realised he'd left them all at home.

"But where are they all coming from?" frowned Casper.

As if to answer that question, two familiar hens picked their way out from a shadowed corner across the eggy floor. Their feathers were threadbare and they had thick leather collars round their tiny necks, but there was no mistaking their grand red wattles and rusty feathers.

"Mavis? Bessie? My girls?" Lamp's lip quivered.

Mavis clucked the saddest cluck Casper had ever heard.

"It's OK, girlies," said Lamp. "I'll get those collars off." He crunched across the eggs, but the hens cowered away from his hands, back towards the shadows.

"What's wrong? It's me, remember? Old cousin Lamp?"

Bessie popped out an egg and clucked apologetically. Mavis cawed and popped one out as well.

Mavis and Bessie. Here. Laying eggs. But that means... Casper's jaw dropped as the answers to his questions plopped into his head like eggs plopping out of a chicken.

"Boys, we're wasting time." Julius was hopping up and down by the door. "You've got to come outside."

"It's the chickens!" gasped Casper. "It's the

chickens and their eggs!"

Julius shook his head. "Right, but I do need you outside, Casp. It's a bit of an emergency."

"Free omelette for every customer and they all turn clever. Lamp eats more eggs than anyone and he's the biggest genius this side of Einstein!"

"But we've gone through this," said Lamp. "I was getting brainy *before* the bistro opened."

"But you were eating omelettes on Monday morning!" Casper clicked his fingers. "Omelettes from those hens."

Lamp looked from Casper's pointing finger to Mavis and Bessie, and then back to Casper's finger. "You don't think… all these eggs…"

Mavis laid three eggs in one plop.

"But they've hardly been laying any eggs at all," objected Lamp.

"That's what we thought. I'll bet they've laid as many as usual, only Jean-Claude's been stealing them. I saw him steal all sorts of things on Tuesday. Would've been easy to pop over and nick a dozen eggs each day. Soon he'd have, well, this many."

Julius was pacing in circles. "Boys, as much as I love chatting about livestock, *we really have to go*."

"Dad. This is important." Casper turned back to face Lamp. "Look, Jean-Claude's been lurking around the village for a while now, but can you remember when he arrived?"

"Maybe two months ago. Shortly before Mavis and Bessie arrived... Oh dear."

"Oh, I am *so* stupid! What if they're Jean-Claude's hens, Lamp? What if Jean-Claude came to Corne-on-the-Kobb with his plan and his hens, spotted your potential and gave you Mavis and Bessie so you'd have a head start? You'd eat their eggs and start getting brainy even earlier than the rest of us."

"But they're my cousins," whimpered Lamp. "The tags on their necks said so."

"They're not your cousins. Those are French hens, Lamp."

"Oh," Lamp's lip quivered. "French? S'pose that explains why I could never understand them."

"You were Jean-Claude's first test-subject and it worked. How he got the hens laying clever eggs, we'll never know. Feeding them books? Sending them off to school? Probably something cruel, knowing him."

"Poor chickies." Lamp tickled Mavis's head.

"Guys," Julius looked up at the clock with desperate eyes. "It's good that you've solved it, but come outside and you'll see we've got bigger fish to fry."

This made no sense. "What's the hurry? It's only seven o'clock. Why are you even up this early?"

"Early? It's seven in the evening!" cried Julius.

"And I'm supposed to be serving food!"

"*What?*" Any remaining joy slipped off Casper's face. "The evening?"

"Yes! Evening, with the cook-off, in the square. Didn't you wonder why the kitchen was so empty?"

"No, I mean, I noticed, but—"

"This was the first time Jean-Claude left the kitchen, my only chance to rescue you before the cook-off. I had to leave Amanda alone with my food to come and find you. I need your help, Casp. This is desperate. *Come on!*" Julius dashed from the kitchen, Casper and Lamp hot on his heels. They danced through the empty tables of *Bistro D'Escargot* and pulled open the door, and the sound from the square hit them full in the face, like a frying pan of noise.

The cook-off had begun.

Chapter 14

Brain Food

The square was packed; let's just get that straight. Every single villager of Corne-on-the-Kobb had turned up at least twice to see the grand cook-off. The pigeons were out in force, perching on both the statue and the real head of Mayor Rattsbulge. Some outsiders were here too – muddy yokels from Little Grimston and snooty aristocrats from Upper Crustenbury – all scrabbling about and falling over and getting tangled up with each other.

To the left of the square, in front of the pub, a long trestle table had been set up to hold all of Jean-Claude's equipment (most of which Lamp had invented): the Fry-Frencher, the Steam-powered Casserole, the spinny thing that turned bricks into chocolate mousse and, of course, the wheezing, sneezing, tartan Omelette Gun, which floated wobblily above the heads of the villagers and screeched like a burst Cuddles.

There stood Jean-Claude D'Escargot, the chef who couldn't cook, proud in his new chef whites and enormous puffy chef's hat. A huge chunk of the crowd watched him work with adoring *oohs* and *aahs* as he pretended to cook, lifting and putting down a knife or turning a tap on.

None of the crowd could get near to Jean-

Claude's machines, however, owing to the four enormous bollards that separated his tables from the rest of the square. Those bollards had pale-blue tracksuits and hairy arms and spotty bruised faces. And worst of all, those bollards had names. Casper tried to say those names aloud, but his throat felt as dry as dust. *Bash*, he thought, *Clobber, Spit and Pinchnurse. The Brewster brothers*.

"He p-p-paid them in l-lunch m-money."

Little Snivel Brewster had crept up behind the boys. He wore a tiny version of the very same tracksuit his brothers had on and a grimace that said, *You've lost*.

"I've b-been to your t-t-table. She's serving b-bowls of t-tap water. S-says it's the only f-fing she c-can c-cook."

"Oh, cripes," cried Julius. "Amanda!" He

launched off towards a long table draped with a Union Jack, set up outside the front door of The Battered Cod. This side of the square was empty, apart from Amanda and Cuddles Candlewacks and three pigeons queuing for a bowl of water. Cuddles sat on a stack of plates, gnawing on some fingers, while Amanda flustered about as if she was running a country.

"Just a minute!" Amanda cried, desperately sloshing the contents of her water jug with the wrong end of a wooden spoon. "I can't keep up with all these orders."

"Amanda, darling. What about the *Crown Jewels Kebabs? Steak 'n' Kidney Pies?* Those *Bulldog Toffees* I boiled up?" Julius looked like he might pull his few remaining hairs out. "Tell me you've been selling the *Jellied Eels*, Amanda."

"But I like water!" sang Amanda.

Casper looked from his dad's empty table to the swarm of brainiacs surrounding Jean-Claude's, and felt his heart sink. This cook-off was more one-sided than last year's Kobb Valley Bodybuilders versus Pensioners Rugby Match, where the pensioners shuffled off halfway through to watch *Antiques Attic*.

Anemonie Blight's pointy black shoes clicked on the cobbles as she skipped past. "Candlewacks is leaving home!" she sang. "Candlewacks is leaving home! Pack your bags, loser! Need help with the bus fare?" The point of her nose wrinkled as she flicked a single penny piece at Casper and skipped away.

BOOM!

Across the square, green confetti filled the air

and the crowd cheered.

"That's my Omlit Gun," puffed Lamp proudly. "Jean-Claude would be nothing without it."

"Yeah," sighed Casper. "And with it, he's everything. But hang on… that's exactly it!"

"It is?" said Lamp.

"Just like you said – he'd be nothing without all your inventions. He relies on them to win. All we have to do is destroy those machines and Dad can't lose!"

Lamp chuckled. "Oh, Casper, you are silly sometimes."

"N-n-no," muttered Snivel, "h-he's right."

Lamp grinned at Snivel, and then at Casper, and then noticed neither was grinning back. He put the grin in his pocket for later and replaced it with a wide-eyed look of horror. "But… I made them.

They're mine and I made them."

"If we let Jean-Claude win, I have to leave the village. For ever. Would you prefer that?"

It was obviously a hard decision. Lamp looked Casper up and down and did some counting in his head. "S'pose I could make some more. But do you have to kill them?"

"There's no other way. Sorry, Lamp." Casper steadied his nerves with a few deep breaths. "Right. Dad, get some food ready. If this goes according to plan, you'll have a couple of hundred hungry villagers to feed."

"I can do that," nodded Julius.

"Snivel, Lamp – you need to distract the Brewsters."

"I'll c-call them ugly," said Snivel.

"I'll teach them the particulars of Fermat's Last

Theorem!" cheered Lamp.

Casper grabbed the jug of water. "And I'll deal with the machines. This should short the circuits. Good luck, chaps."

Lamp saluted.

Snivel itched his face.

"Casper," said Amanda, "why are you wearing my dress?"

The crowd was thick near Jean-Claude's table, so nobody saw the three approach, but Snivel got the Brewsters' attention quickly enough.

"Hey! B-Bash!" Snivel shouted, his squeaky voice carrying over the crowd with surprising power. "You got a f-face like a d-donkey's armpit."

Bash spun round, spotted his little brother and snarled. Snivel didn't wait a second longer than he had to; he darted away between two men in anoraks, but Bash caught the scent and blitzed straight after him with fists raised. Never one to miss out on a fight, Pinchnurse followed behind. Meanwhile Spit and Clobber scratched their buzz-cut heads and nibbled their lips at the mathematical conundrums Lamp was posing. With Jean-Claude pretending to fricassee some rabbit loin for the baying crowd, not a soul saw Casper steal behind the line of tables with his water jug.

Crouching, Casper reached up and poured a splosh of water into the top of a jiggling pink laundry basket.

TSSSSSS.

Squelches of unbaked bread seeped through its holes and the jiggling stopped. Next was a spaghetti-stretching mechanical monkey.

SHHHHKNK.

The monkey's arms dropped and the spaghetti flopped to the table.

GLUGLUGLUG... BONK.

There went the coconut-juicer.

SSSSPNTBLOLOLOING.

Hundreds of champagne jellies bounced to the cobbles.

FIZZZ-WHEEE.

Whatever that one used to be, it was now purple and broken.

"Lunch munny."

Casper frowned. That was an odd noise for a machine to make. He poured a little more water on.

"Lunch munny."

And then Casper felt the hot-tuna breath on the back of his neck and realised his mistake.

Jean-Claude looked round from his chopping board. "What is going on?" His rubbery face curled with displeasure as it met Casper's, and his cigarette dropped hissing to the floor. "*Boy.* I thought I was rid of you, but 'ere you are, getting in my way once more. You are like a boomerang and I 'ave had enough of you. Brewsters? Throw him away! And zis time, make sure he won't come back!"

"RETREAT!" Casper yelled, diving to his left just as a brutish fist whooshed past his head. He leapt up, spun round and ran straight back under Bash Brewster's outstretched arm into the crowd.

"D-did you do it?" Snivel was right by him, ducking daintily through the pack of villagers.

"Some, but not enough." Casper looked back to see only six of the thirty or so machines pluming smoke.

"S-sorry. B-bash forgot he was ch-chasing me and went b-b-back. I c-can't keep them away for l-long enough."

Lamp stood under Mayor Rattsbulge's statue nursing a dead arm. "They didn't agree with Fermat's conclusion, Casper," he said, prodding the arm gently. "Wakey wakey."

"Six machines down at the cost of one arm and very nearly my head. We need a new tactic." Casper gritted his teeth. "Long-range attack. Everyone, empty your pockets!"

Casper had some fluff, a paper clip and the ring pull from a tin of peaches. Snivel had a packet of plasters and a comfort blanket. Lamp had twenty-eight-and-a-half eggs.

"Where do you keep all those?" asked Casper, amazed.

Lamp tapped his nose. "Secret pockets," he said. "I sewn them in."

"But that's perfect! Who's got good aim?"

Snivel shook his head.

Lamp shrugged.

"Fine. I'll give it a go," Casper grunted. "If I can get an egg in the works, it'll clog up all the machinery. We've got twenty-eight eggs and twenty-four machines to hit. Should be fine." His stomach gurgled. Fifteen metres away sat the line of Lamp's machines, the wheezing Omelette Gun right in the middle. In front, the four Brewsters towered protectively above the crowd. Casper flicked the hair from his eyes and grabbed an egg. "Watch this."

The egg left his hand cleanly, spinning as it cleared the heads of the nearest villagers and soared into the sky. Up it flew, up and up, until it seemed to hang in the air above Jean-Claude's table. But the egg had veered too far to the left, and as it began to plummet, Casper saw he'd pitched too short. It dropped like a stone, flipping and wobbling until it landed with an ominous crack… on the shoulder of Bash Brewster's tracksuit.

Bash looked at the yolk running down his front, and then up at the crowd. "Oo did dat?" he roared, teeth bared, and without waiting for an answer, he reached behind him and flung the first thing to hand at the villagers. A clump of boiled rice struck Sandy Landscape's cheek.

"Oy there!" Sandy lashed out with a carrot, whipping about and catching the hairs of Spit Brewster's nose. Spit roared in indignation and started lobbing boiled tomatoes, which struck a dozen screaming faces as they hailed down on the crowd. Clemmie Answorth grabbed a bucket of mayonnaise and a ladle to flick it with, while Mayor Rattsbulge had drawn two double-barrelled sausages from his holster.

"FOOD FIGHT!" the mayor roared as he unloaded the first sausage at Mitch McMassive.

"*Non!* Do ze stopping!" yelped Jean-Claude as a strawberry meringue exploded by his feet and his Soufflé Puffer toppled to the ground. A volley of olives followed the meringue, uprooting two more of Lamp's nearby inventions and knocking off Jean-Claude's hat. "My machines! You are ruining zem!"

Casper's mouth gaped open. "I missed, but… I hit!" The food fight was in full fling now, and the biggest casualties were the delicate inventions, their intricate wiring now spattered with spinach and buttercream, their circuits fizzing from the red wine *jus* that rained from the sky. Grabbing two more eggs, he flung one into the crowd and cracked the second over Mrs Trimble's head.

Anemonie had joined in by now, jabbing at nearby brainiacs with the spiky end of a pineapple, and Milly and Milly Mollyband had scaled Mayor Rattsbulge's statue and were taking potshots with seedless grapes.

Casper cackled with delight as he shielded himself from a treacle tart and threw more eggs. Snivel ducked deftly when Sandy Landscape lunged at him with a carrot, then giggled and introduced the gardener's bald spot to an egg.

"Stop it!" shouted Lamp. "Those eggs are mine!"

The hideous wheeze of the Omelette Gun screeched above the crowd noise, and those not yet blinded looked round to see Jean-Claude, the vacuum-cleaner neck under his arm, loosing omelettes at approaching villagers.

"Get back!" he roared. "Ze machines must not be 'armed!"

An omelette splattered Anemonie in the face, and by the time it slid off, she was already reciting Shakespeare.

The omelettes had grounded ten villagers, what with the force that Jean-Claude fired them. Casper took Lamp's last two eggs and danced forward, one in each hand. He dodged behind Mayor Rattsbulge to avoid the omelette that soared towards him and threw an egg right back, but its flight path met that of a chocolate log and they both exploded, spattering their innards across the crowd.

Casper dived for the cobbles and held his breath. He could feel the cold eggy slop hitting his head, but as long as it didn't touch his mouth, he knew he'd be fine. Jean-Claude was close – Casper could hear the bagpipes and smell the garlic.

All around the Frenchman, the remains of Lamp's inventions hissed and sizzled. One thing was for sure– he'd be cooking no more food tonight.

"Give up, Jean-Claude!" cried Casper, hiding his face behind a poppadom. "You've lost! Your machines are ruined!"

"Ah, *non*. Not all of zem!"

FLOOM.

Casper dived for the cobbles once more, the omelette missing him by centimetres. He peeked up in time to see that it had hit Bash Brewster, and that he'd responded with the closest bit of food to hand, which just happened to be

Mitch McMassive. Squealing, Mitch spun through the air towards Jean-Claude's table and Casper had to duck again, but Mitch's squeak and a hideous burp from the bagpipes told Casper all he needed to know. Direct hit.

"*NON!*" roared Jean-Claude. "My machine! You fool!"

"Sorry," said Mitch. "I've got some tape at home." But the damage was done. Round the tiny barman, the Omelette Gun deflated and died, screaming its last sad notes through a dozen punctures. The last invention was broken – Jean-Claude was beaten.

"But… but…" The Frenchman's mouth pursed in horror, and then he saw Casper. "Heh." His face tightened. "You think you are so clever, boy?"

"Give up, Jean-Claude."

"Never! If I am going down, I will take your fazzer wiz me!"

"What d'you mean? My dad's fine!"

But as Jean-Claude vaulted over the table and bustled through the crowd, Casper had doubts. "Where are you going? Come back and give yourself up!" Casper tried to push after him, but the gaps in the crowd closed themselves up as soon as they'd opened. Soon he was face to face with Betty Woons and two cream pies, but he only managed to dodge one of them.

As he fell, bodies piled on top, squelching and yelping.

"Stop it now!" Casper yelled, wriggling under the mass of three brawling villagers. "The fight's over. We've won! We need to get Jean-Claude!"

But everybody's ears were filled with custard.

"Let me go!" He wrenched free and pushed the villagers aside, climbing upwards and scraping sauce from his dress.

Across the square, some huge commotion had caught the villagers' eyes. The crowd was too dense to see what was causing the ruckus, so Casper pushed forward, worried at how close it was to Julius's table. And then he saw them – two men locked in a heated sword fight.

"Combat!" The brainiacs screamed with excitement.

One of the sword-fighting men was French and stumpy; the other tall and balding. Their swords were producing quite a few crumbs. In fact, they weren't strictly *sword* fighting at all because for that you'd need swords. And those weren't swords. They were *baguettes*.

Chapter 15

Breaking Bread

"Dad?" Casper bellowed. "What's happening?"

Jean-Claude growled at the intrusion and stabbed at Julius's chest, missing, but forcing him back.

"Casper—"

CLOB.

Jean-Claude's loaf struck Julius round the head and he clattered to the floor in a bread-clobbered heap.

"DAD!"

The crowd let out a disappointed sigh.

"Over already?" moaned Audrey Snugglepuss. "But I so love a good duel."

"Oh, it's not over." Anger swelled in Casper's belly as he ran to his defeated father, lying there crummy and winded. He leant down to pick up Julius's loaf, not once taking his eyes off the villain before him. "Jean-Claude D'Escargot, you've messed with the wrong village."

"Bah." The Frenchman spat at the ground and sneered through his grubby teeth. "Do not make me do ze laughing, boy. Get out of my way. I will be finishing off your fazzer."

"I'm not moving." Casper's baguette trembled. "You've come here for revenge, but my dad owes you nothing. How many chefs' careers have you ruined with bad reviews, huh? Hundreds? Even thousands? My dad was just the first to stand up for himself. You think you can ruin my dad's life just because you're too high and mighty to write a proper review? You didn't even taste his food!"

"He cheated me wiz his English tricks!" Jean-Claude roared. "He made me ze fool! I will be paying him back, if it's ze last thing I do." With his free hand, Jean-Claude fumbled for a cigarette from a pack in his pocket, pursing it between his rubbery lips as he lit it.

"You'll have to get past *me*." Casper didn't know what he was doing. He didn't even know if he was holding his baguette the right way round. But he couldn't fail now. The consequences would be too dire.

"*Hergh*." Jean-Claude coughed, letting the cigarette flop to the side of his mouth. "Zen DIE!" He charged, slashing his baguette straight at Casper's neck. Casper parried the blow by instinct, but lost his footing and stumbled backwards. Instantly Jean-Claude was on him again, jabbing from above and then lunging at Casper's chest. Casper fell back further, dodging his blows, but losing vital ground.

The crowd began to chant, but what they said was too indistinct for Casper to hear.

FWOOSH.

The baguette whistled past Casper's head, but he ducked just in time.

"You cannot do ze winning, boy."

The crowd chanted, every mouth repeating the same words, but Casper still couldn't make out what they were saying.

"Stop that!" he yelled between frenzied bats of his baguette. "It's distracting."

Lamp appeared by his ear. "It's easy for us, Casper." He tapped his brain. "Brainiacs, you see. Just copy what we say and you can't lose. Speak up, everyone!"

The villagers chanted more loudly. "Lunge! Parry! Lunge! *Riposte!*" they cried, and Casper did his best to follow their instructions.

"Zey cannot help you!" Jean-Claude beat back Casper's attack with ease. "I 'ave fed their minds with intelligence, not sword skill."

"Jump!" cried the crowd and Casper did so, just as Jean-Claude swiped at Casper's feet.

"You're wrong, sir," said Lamp. Fencing's easy when you know what the other guy's going to do next. It's a bit like chess."

"Pah! As if you know zat."

"Parry! Parry! Feint! Stab!"

Casper didn't know what some of those moves were, but he tried his best and it *was* forcing Jean-Claude backwards.

"Lunge! Riposte! Lunge! *Flèche!*"

"What's *flèche*?" Casper had to guess, swinging his baguette twice round his head. Evidently he was wrong because he found himself wide open. Jean-Claude didn't need a second opportunity; he charged and struck hard on Casper's chest. The cobbles met his fall, knocking the wind from his fingers and the baguette from his lungs (or was it the other way round?).

A gasp rose from the crowd, followed by deathly silence.

Jean-Claude loomed over Casper. He pressed his crust firmly to his victim's neck. "You lose, boy. I am ze last man standing. Victory, she is mine."

"Oh yeah?" It was a struggle to speak with the bread pressing against Casper's windpipe, but he had nothing left to lose. "I thought this was a cook-off. If you're the winner, where's your food to show for it?"

"You destroyed it wiz your petty little food fight."

"Then cook some more!"

"*Non!* I will not!" Jean-Claude raised his baguette.

"Tell them why not, Jean-Claude." Casper turned his head to face the crowd. "They deserve to know. Why can't you cook any more?"

The Frenchman spluttered. "It… er… IT DOES NOT MATTER." He raised the baguette further, ready to strike.

But Casper hadn't finished. "It's because you can't cook! Admit it! You couldn't make toast if your head was a toaster!"

"Fine. I cannot do ze cooking! What does it matter? It ends the same for you, boy." He grinned his black-toothed grin.

"You'll never get away with this, Jean-Claude," said Casper helplessly.

Jean-Claude tipped his head back and laughed, a vile, phlegmy, dirty laugh that echoed round the square and made Ted Treadington cry. "Who will be stopping me? Huh?" He swung his baguette menacingly and the crowd shifted backwards. "*Au revoir*, boy," snickered Jean-Claude. He raised the baguette once more, this time bringing it crashing down.

Casper scrunched his eyes shut, clenched his teeth. This was it…

SPONK.

He held his breath, but the hit never came.

Something had gone *SPONK*, but it wasn't him. He dared to open an eye. The man standing over him was considerably larger than Jean-Claude D'Escargot. In his outstretched hand was a massive Cumberland sausage. Casper's gaze followed the flabby hand that held it, to a purple mayoral gown, to a broad gold medallion, to sixteen trembling chins, to the furious face of Mayor Rattsbulge, his lip curled in anger.

"Whu…?" was all that Casper could manage. He felt something lying across his feet, heavy like a stocking at Christmas. He lifted his aching head, but found no presents. Jean-Claude lay face down on the cobbles, out cold after a sausage shot to the temple.

"He… couldn't… even… *cook*?" wobbled Mayor Rattsbulge, sneering down at the motionless Frenchman.

"He tricked you all into doing it for him," muttered Casper, cool relief coursing through his veins.

"HOW DARE HE!" Colour flushed back through the mayor's face. "*A chef who can't cook? Why, that's like… a mayor who can't raise taxes.*" A shudder travelled through the whole of his gigantic body, finishing with a wild shake of his jowels. "This imposter will forfeit his place in the cook-off at once, and will henceforth be banished from Corne-on-the-Kobb. You, men, GET HIM OUT OF MY SIGHT!"

The crowd cheered and Casper would've leapt up and kissed the mayor had he not been exhausted to his bones and wearing a dress. Closing his eyes, he rested his head back on the cobbles and let out a long sigh. It was over. Jean-Claude had been beaten and Julius got to keep his restaurant at the price of one bread shot to the head. Luckily, Casper knew his father would be fine after a cup of tea and a drop of brandy – he'd had worse, after all; Julius fell off the roof three times when fixing the aerial and survived to tell the tale.

In the meantime, Jean-Claude gurgled as Bash Brewster hoisted him over one shoulder. "Where's we takin' 'im?"

"Search me," shrugged Mayor Rattsbulge. "What's it say on his label?"

"He's from France," murmured Casper from his horizontal position on the cobbles. "Are you going that way?"

"France?" Bash chewed over the word as if

he'd never heard it before.

"Chip shop's near France, innit?" said Clobber.

"We's deffo goin' chip shop," grinned Spit.

"We'll take 'im," said Bash. "Maybe 'e's got lunch munny."

"He's yours," announced Mayor Rattsbulge dismissively. "Just take him away."

The four brothers tromped away across the square, Jean-Claude flopping limply up and down in time with their footsteps. They tromped down the road, past the pelican crossing and off into the sunset.

Snivel shuffled forward and hovered close to Casper. "D-d'you fink they'll m-make it to F-france?"

"Doubt it," grimaced Casper, pulling himself up painfully to a standing position. "They'll probably forget where they're going round the next corner. And I wouldn't want to be them when Jean-Claude wakes up. Right mood he'll be in."

"M-maybe they need a n-navigator," said Snivel. "I'm g-good with maps."

"That's an idea."

"Ooh! And you can feed him a omlit if he gets rowdy," suggested Lamp, skipping out from the doorway of *Bistro D'Escargot* flanked by Mavis and Bessie, free from collars and flapping the cobwebs off their wings. "Nice bit of brains should calm him down, get him thinking rationally. Want to take the girls?"

"Y-yeah. All right." Snivel puffed up his chest proudly. "If they'll c-come."

As if on cue, Mavis and Bessie strutted over to peck at the youngest Brewster's feet, and for the first time since Casper had known him, Snivel looked genuinely happy.

"Go and find your brothers, Snivel," said Casper. "Keep 'em in line!"

"W-will do!" He did a little salute. "C-come on, ladies." He trotted off at a pace in the same direction as the Brewsters. Mavis and Bessie flapped along beside him, and before long they were out of sight.

Back in the square, Lamp had gone cross-eyed. "Casper, there's something dongly on my face."

Casper frowned. "That's your nose."

"My nose. I knew that." Lamp shuffled awkwardly. "Nose."

"Is everything all right?"

"Casper, I think my brains is running out. I used to know about noses and stuff, but now

I can't remember."

Casper felt his pulse surge. Could it possibly be? He had to check. "What's four plus three?"

"Um," Lamp chewed his lip. "Thursday?"

"Wrong!" Casper had never been so happy to hear a wrong answer, but he couldn't look too happy, for Lamp's sake. He lent his friend a comforting arm. "Bad news, Lamp. I think the eggs are wearing off."

Lamp gave a sorrowful sniff.

"It's OK. I like you best when you're not a brainiac."

"Thanks, Casper." Lamp grinned. "What's a brainiac?"

All around them, villagers were coming to their senses.

"Must've been something in those burgers," mumbled Mayor Rattsbulge.

"Why's I holdin' a calculator?" asked Sandy Landscape, and then he went off to plant it.

Down on the cobbles, Julius stirred.

"Dad!"

"Casp? That you?"

Casper leant down beside his father. "Yeah, I'm here. You took a serious bread shot back there. Thought I'd lost you."

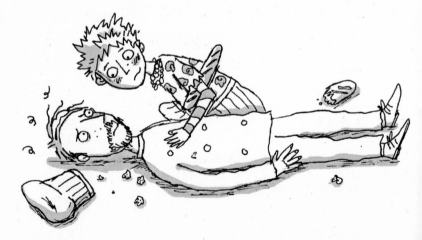

"Urgh, my head. Did you… Is he gone?"

"We got him. I'm fine. So're Mum and Cuddles."

Across the square, Amanda was trying to separate Cuddles from the three cats she was currently trying to swallow.

"You beat him?"

"Sort of," Casper nodded. "Lamp helped."

"My little swordsman. Some day you'll be as good as your old man. I'm proud of you, Casp." Julius closed his eyes. "You know, I saw my life flash before my eyes back there."

"Don't think it was your life, Dad. I'm pretty sure it was a baguette."

"Oh. Yeah."

With a screech, Clemmie Answorth tripped over a pigeon and clattered to the cobbles. Things really were back to normal.

"This calls for pie," Mayor Rattsbulge announced. "Everybody, listen up. You're all invited to The Battered Cod for a free meal."

"Are they?" Casper gulped.

The mayor licked his lips. "Hurrah for Julius Candlewacks!"

"Hurrah for Julius Candlewacks!" the crowd cheered.

"Hurrah for me?" Julius mumbled, but he was drowned out by the stampede of feet as every single idiot in Corne-on-the-Kobb piled into The Battered Cod.

Ting-a-ling.

Mr Flanty's Pi Song

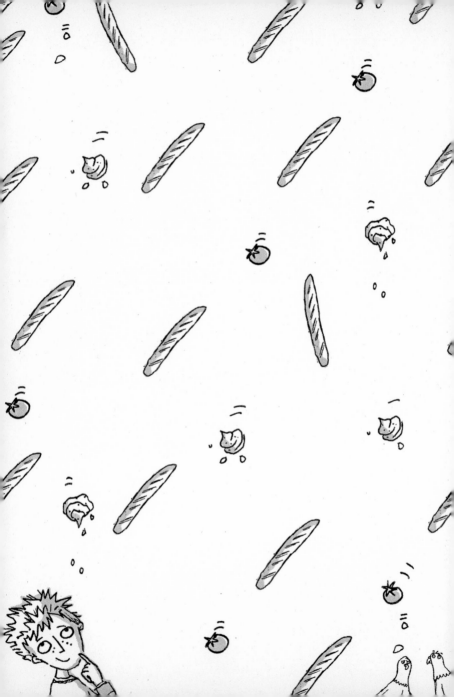